The Ultimate Betrayal

Lock Down Publications

Presents

The Ultimate Betrayal

A Novel by *Phoenix*

Lock Down Publications

P.O. Box 1482
Pine Lake, Ga 30072-1482

Lock Down Publications
Email: l.amthe1phoenix@gmail.com
Facebook: Phoenix Thewriter
Like our page on Facebook: Lock Down Publications @
www.facebook.com/lockdownpublications.ldp
Cover design and layout by: **Dynasty's Cover Me**
Book interior design by: **Shawn Walker**
Edited by: **Mia Rucker**

Phoenix

Chapter 1

I met Amir when I was seventeen at his twenty-first birthday party. Amir and Nique, my best friend, are first cousins and their birthdays are three days apart, so technically it was *their* twenty-first birthday party. Anyway, I was watching him and fantasizing about all the things I wanted him to do to me when someone put their hands over my eyes and said, "Wipe the drool off your chin, bitch!"

Laughing, I turned around and punched Nique playfully in the arm. "Shut up, bitch, I wasn't drooling. Happy birthday," I said as I pinned a crisp Benji on her shirt. Nique and I were taking shots and dancing, enjoying ourselves.

After a while, we decided to take a breather and catch up. While we were talking, Amir and Cas walked up. We exchanged greetings and then Cas whisked Nique off to the dance floor.

So there I was alone with Amir for the first time. He was so breathtaking, the way his six-foot nine-inch muscular frame towered over me. I was in awe just being near him, inhaling his intoxicating scent. I was lost in a daydream, imagining all of the nasty things I wanted him to do to me.

Whew, I exhaled and fanned myself trying to shake those thoughts from my mind and ignore the throbbing of my clit. I was dancing in place to the slow song that was playing when he put his arm around my waist and whispered, "Ma, I won't bite you, not unless you want me to."

He led me to the dance floor. We slow danced for three songs before we were interrupted by some chick that would later become a thorn in my side.

"*Excuse me,* are you serious right now, Amir?" the girl said.

"Man, g'on wit the bullshit, Keta." Amir sighed and turned around.

"You got me fucked up. How you gon' disrespect me like that?" she said as she eyeballed me.

"Disrespect you? *Who* the fuck are you to disrespect? Be clear on this, Keta, we are just *fucking.* That's it and that's all. So whatever you thought this was, unthink that shit," he gritted.

"Really, Amir, that's how you playing it?" Keta questioned as she stepped back in shock.

"It is what it is. You aren't my girl anymore. Stop embarrassing yourself," he said

"Whatever, Amir, I'm ready to go *now,*" she said as she eye balled me.

"It looks like you have some business to handle. Thanks for the dance. Happy birthday," I said as I walked away.

"I am about to finish enjoying *my* party. You're more than welcome to stay. But if you leave, thank you for coming," he said as he turned to walk away.

I wasn't for the drama and shit so I left him to handle his issue. *He isn't my man, we were just dancing. But if the bitch has beef, she knows where to find me,* I thought as I went to go mingle.

I found a secluded spot to get myself together. *I don't even know why I am tripping,* I thought as I watched Nique and Cas cupcake. Then Amir walked up, interrupting their moment.

"Damn, get a room," said Amir, laughing.

"Shut up, Mir. Where my girl at?" Nique asked, amused.

"Bae, she shot his ass down. That's why he over here fucking up our groove," Cas said, chuckling.

"Nigga, I don't get shot down. I am too damn handsome for

that," Amir said with a confident grin.

"Handsome, where? Boy, stop, your ugly ass ran her off," Nique said, giggling.

"Shut up, Nique. Have you seen her, tho?" Amir said, laughing slightly.

"We left her with you. You fucked up already, huh?" Cas said.

"Man, Keta ass walked up spazzing on a nigga. Then shorty hit me wit some fly shit and walked away," Amir sighed.

"What, Nique?" Amir asked, noticing Nique's questioning expression.

"Nothing. I'm goin' to go find my girl, if she is still here. But your ass better tell ya rat and her hoe crew this ain't what they want," Nique said as she walked off.

I saw Nique walk off mumbling to herself. I figured Amir must have told her what happened, which wasn't a big deal to me. *Or was it?* I wondered as I shot her a text telling her I was leaving and that I would get up with her tomorrow.

I was walking to my car, minding my business, when I heard a voice behind me. *Here goes the bullshit,* I thought as I slipped out of my shoes.

"Yea, bitch, you better be heading home. The street lights are on." Keta laughed as she gave a few girls around her high fives.

"Is that the best you can come with, sweetie?" I asked as I smirked. I hoped she didn't think I was going to run because she had that whack ass crew with her.

"Bitch, stay the fuck away from Amir," Keta yelled as she stepped into my face.

I just looked her in the eyes and smirked because if this bitch was really 'bout it, she would have hit me. I saw the fear in her eyes as I watched her try to figure out my next move.

"*Keta,* don't fucking touch her. Take your ass home *now,*" Amir gritted.

"Looks like the captain came to save his hoe," Keta said

"The only hoe out here is you. So you better be a good hoe and do as you're told," I said.

"You taking up for this bitch, Amir?" Keta asked as she reached out to slap Amir.

Grabbing her wrist and pulling her close to him, Amir harshly whispered in her ear. "Bitch, if you ever try that shit again, you are gonna have to learn how to eat with your feet. Now take your ass the fuck home," Amir gritted as he released her wrist and walked away.

I knew the shit was far from over. I just stood there making sure she followed orders because bitches like her couldn't be trusted.

I finally turned to walk away, but Amir reached out and gently grabbed my arm.

"Hey, are you good?" Amir asked.

"I am fine. Just keep your hoes in line," I said to him as I removed his hand and proceeded to walk to my car.

Falling in step with me, he said, "Amina, I apologize about all that. She is not my girl."

"It's cool. Well, I am going to get going, enjoy the rest of your party," I said as I started to open my car door.

"Well, can I get your number so I can make it up to you over breakfast or lunch, hell maybe even dinner?" Amir laughed.

"I don't know," I smirked and gave him the side eye.

"Come on, baby girl, don't make me beg," he said as he tried to hand me his phone.

"You're sexy when you beg," I smirked as we exchanged

phones.

"Be safe, baby girl, and text me so that I know you made it home," Amir said as he closed my door.

I held my composure as I backed out of the space because he was watching me. *Oh my god, oh my god, I touched his phone. He has my number. Keta better enjoy that dick tonight 'cause I am about to shut shit down,* I said to myself as I went through the stop sign. The ride home usually took ten minutes, but it seemed like I got home faster. I felt like I was floating when I got out the car. When I got in the house, I quickly shot Amir a text letting him know I made it home. Then I hopped in the shower.

I usually sleep in on Saturday but I was awakened by the ringing of my phone. I tried so hard to ignore it, but it seemed as if it didn't want to stop ringing.

"Helllooo," I groggily spoke.

"Wake up, beautiful. Be ready in an hour, baby girl, I am taking you to breakfast," Amir stated. He sounded as if he was wide awake.

The sound of his voice instantly caused a flood in my panties. *Damn, why does he even sound sexy in the morning?* I thought.

"What if I say no? What time is it? Why are you up?" I sassily asked.

"The early bird catches the worm. It is eight o' clock, baby girl. I will see you in an hour," Amir stated, and then ended the call.

Who the hell does he think he is? I asked myself as I tossed my legs over the side of my bed. I hopped up and jumped in the shower. I decided that I was going to dress down today, so I put on black stone wash skinny jeans, a fitted black V-neck tee, and some red chucks. I put on some gold accessories, light makeup, and I pulled my hair up into a high ponytail. I had fifteen minutes to spare, so I hit Nique up to kill time.

"Good morning, boo. Are you good? Amir told me what happened," Nique said.

"Girl, yeah, I'm fine. She called herself approaching me when I was leaving but Amir saved her from the ass whooping she was about to receive," I said.

"Girl, Keta ain't 'bout nothing. Soo why are you up so early on this beautiful *Saturday* morning?" Nique laughed.

"I have a date, which I am sure you already know about, if you must know, nosey," I laughed

"Girllll, you made his day. He had me freshen up his line up like it wasn't already on point," Nique laughed.

"His line up stay fresh. He is high maintenance. Girl he just walked up so I will call you later."

"Okay, behave young lady and have fun," she laughed and ended the call.

Taking a deep breath, I opened the door to see a smiling Amir.

"Hey, beautiful, are you ready?" Amir said as he held his hand out.

I placed my hand in his. "Yes, I'm ready," I said as I closed and locked the door to my house.

Chapter 2

Once we reached his black '85 Grand National, he opened the door for me and then he went around and got in. I was admiring the custom-made red leather bucket seats. The leather was so soft. When he turned the car on, I was surprised to hear the smooth voice of Sade singing.

"What you know about Sade?" I smirked.

"What you mean? I love Sade, *cherish the day,*" Amir sang.

"Please let her sing. I didn't expect to hear this," I laughed.

He just looked at me and smirked as we rode in a comfortable silence.

When we arrived at Mimosa, I was in awe of the scenery. Mimosa was off the beaten path, hidden behind a vast amount of lush trees. I had always dreamed of going there. The tall oak trees and the lake gave you a serene country vibe. I could spend all day there. I am such a country girl at heart. I was so lost in my daydream that I didn't realize we stopped.

"A penny for your thoughts, love," Amir said as he waved his hand in my face.

"I'm sorry I was just taking in the scenery," I blushed.

"I know. I am breathtaking, huh?" he laughed.

"Whatever," I said as I placed my hand in his and stepped out of the car.

He handed the keys to the valet and we walked towards the lake.

"So, Miss Amina, when were you going to tell me that you had a crush on me?" Amir asked.

"I don't know what you're talking about," I said.

Phoenix

"Don't play shy with me. Keep that shit real. I peep how you look at me when I come around," Amir said.

"I like you, but I know that I am too young for you. I don't handle rejection well so I didn't want to be embarrassed," I blushed and looked away.

Reaching out to lift my chin and turn my face to him, he spoke to me just above a whisper. "Amina, I peeped you, too. You always disappeared before I got a chance to really holla at you. Yeah, you're young but there is something about you," Amir said as he looked into my eyes.

I wanted to give him all of me right there on that bridge, but I am not that type of girl. I needed to be sure he was the one.

"You always come around when I have things to do," I laughed.

"Hmm, what or who has you so busy?" he asked.

"Is that your way of asking do I have a boyfriend? If so, the answer is no. I stay busy with school and work," I said.

"First of all, whether or not you have a boyfriend doesn't matter to me. But if you did, the fact that you're here would tell me that homeboy days are numbered," he stated as he wrapped his arms around my waist.

I leaned into him and enjoyed the feel of his body against mine. I felt his dick slightly jump against the small of my back.

"So, Amir, tell me something I don't know about you," I said as I stepped out of his embrace and started to walk.

"I have my Bachelor's in business and I am thinking about going to get my masters," Amir said.

I tried to hide the shock in my voice when I said, "I didn't know you went to college."

"You thought a nigga was out here dumb doing dirt, huh? Only a few close people know that. I have a rep to uphold out here," he laughed.

He laughed it off, but I knew I offended him. I stopped walking and looked up into his honey colored eyes and said, "Amir I didn't mean to offend you. I'm sorry."

I stood on my tippy toes and lightly pecked his lips. Just as I was about to back away, he pulled me closer and kissed me with so much passion.

Is this happening right now? Oh my god, this is better than I imagined it would be, I thought as a small moan escaped my lips. *I hope he didn't hear that,* I thought as I felt my feet being lowered to the ground. *Damn, he heard it.*

"Was that your stomach, baby girl? Let's go eat," he said as we walked hand in hand back to the restaurant.

Once we were seated, the conversation flowed effortlessly.

"Hi, my name is Melody. I will be your waiter today. Can I start you with an appetizer?" she asked.

"Yes, may I get strawberry crepes for my appetizer? And I will have strawberry lemonade to drink," I spoke flirtatiously.

"And for you, sir?" she blushed.

"I will just have a strawberry lemonade for now," he smiled.

"Okay, I will have your drinks back shortly," Melody said as she sashayed away.

"Let me find out you like girls," Amir laughed.

"*What?* I mean she was a cutie. I seen you checking her out, too," I laughed.

Before he could respond, my crepes and our drinks had arrived.

"Let me know when you're ready to order," she said.

We both just nodded our heads as we looked into each other's eyes. I took a sip of my lemonade.

"Amir, why did you start?" I asked.

"Shit, to be honest with you, I don't really have a reason other than the fact that I am good at it," he stated cockily.

"Naw, seriously, I did it for my mom. Watching her struggle made me take to the streets. She tried to stay strong for me and my brother but I always heard her up late night crying, shit hurt a nigga heart," he stated.

"You have a brother? I never knew that," I asked.

"Yea, his name is Demitri. Nobody really talks about him. My mom sent him away when I was ten," he sadly stated.

I took the moment and leaned over and lightly pecked his lips.

"So tell me about you, baby girl?" he said.

"Well, I am an only child. I am currently a senior and I am also taking classes at Tribeca Community College," I said.

"That much I know. I want to know what you do for fun. What makes you tick?" he asked.

"I like to do many things for fun. I will try anything once, well, almost anything," I giggled.

"What are your plans after graduation?" he said.

"I plan on studying law," I said.

"I have to stay in your good graces. I may need a lawyer one day," he laughed.

"Is everything alright? Are you ready to order?" Melody asked.

"Let me get the T-bone steak, a vegetable omelet, hash browns, and two pancakes," he said.

"And for you, ma'am?" she asked.

"I will have a ham and cheese omelet, two pancakes, and grits," I said.

She took our menus and disappeared. I couldn't take my eyes off her ass until I heard Amir clear his throat.

14

"Sorry, her ass is so captivating," I laughed.

"Why don't you have a man?" he asked.

"Because they only want one thing and I am *not* putting out," I said.

He tried to mask the shock and excitement in his voice when he asked, "Are you a virgin?"

I knew that was coming. I hesitated a little before I answered. I turned to look him in the eye when I said, "Technically yes."

"What do you mean technically?" he asked with a raised brow.

"It means that no man has ever tasted, touched, or seen my goodies," I stated matter-of-factly. "Why are you single, Mr. Carter?" I asked.

Before he was able to answer, the food arrived. We ate in a comfortable silence for a moment, but I wanted an answer to my question.

"I'm waiting," I said.

"I haven't found the one yet, but I think my search will soon be over," he confidently replied.

"Interesting," I said.

We finished our meal.

When the check came, I reached for it but he popped my hand and gave Melody the money.

"Next time it's on me," I said as I got up from the table. Before we walked out, I slipped Melody my number. *She looks like she tastes sweet,* I thought as we hopped in the car.

The whole time we were at Mimosa, his phone was going crazy and I ignored it. But the shit was getting out of control.

"Do you need to get that? I mean they have been calling all morning," I said.

"Naw, baby girl, it ain't nobody important. This is our time," he said as he kissed my hand.

I assumed it was Keta blowing up his phone, but I wasn't too sure. I wasn't about to trip on it, though. He was with me for the moment.

"Are you ready to go home?" he asked.

"No, I am enjoying myself. But if you have something to do, you can drop me off," I said.

"Well, baby girl, just let me know when you are ready to go home," he said as we pulled up at the light

I leaned over and kissed him. I just couldn't get enough of his lips. Our kiss was cut short as horns blared behind us.

Chapter 3

We pulled up at Cas's store. As Amir got out of the car, he told me, "Baby, I will be right back."

He wasn't even in the store for five minutes before drama pulled up.

Keta and her goons came flying into the parking lot. The car was barely stopped completely when Keta hopped out. She tried to open his doors but they were locked, so she went into the store.

Ain't no bitch in my blood. I just refuse to fuss and fight over a man that isn't mine. I am looking too cute to be showing my ass out here. But if these hoes feel froggy, I am going to handle it for sure, I thought.

Her simple ass friends kept trying to look thru the windows to see if anybody was inside but the tint was too dark so they couldn't see me.

I sent Nique a text.

"What you doing?" I texted.

"Shit, 'bout to go see my baby real quick. Are you still with your boo, lol?"

"Girlll, yea, I'm still with my hubby, lol. Let me stop. Yes we are at the store so I will see you when you get here. Oh yea, Keta and her goons are here," I replied.

"A'ight" she replied.

As I put my phone back in my bag, Amir and Keta were coming out of the store.

"Why the fuck have you been ignoring me?" Keta fussed.

"Cause I don't have shit to say to you," he said.

Amir tried to walk away but she grabbed his arm and said,

"You fucked me all night and now you don't have shit to say to *me*. What was all that shit you was saying when you were in it?"

"Keta take your fucking hands off of me," he gritted as he snatched away from her.

In the midst of them arguing, Nique pulled up, hopped out, and said, "Are you good, Mir?"

"Hell yea, he good, bitch. Keep it fucking moving," Keta said.

"Bitch, I am talking to Amir. Don't jump bad cause you with these whack ass bitches," Nique said.

"Everything is good Ni. So what I said some shit in the moment. You sucked my dick so good I would have promised you the world *in that moment*. This is why you will never be nothing more than a nut bitch," he said as he walked away. He hopped in the car and skirted out of the parking lot.

The ride home was silent. I was lost in my thoughts, thinking, *Damn, why does he come with so much drama?*

When we pulled up to my house, there was an awkward silence but my mind was made up. Once I got out of his car, that was it. He looked as if he wanted to say something, but I stopped him before he could start.

"You don't have to apologize. Thanks for breakfast. I really enjoyed myself," I said as I got out of the car.

I walked up on my porch and noticed he was still sitting there. I shrugged it off and walked in the house.

I was worn out so I decided to take a bath. I kept replaying every kiss over and over in my mind.

My hands had just slid under the water when my phone went off.

It was a text message from Melody.

Melody: Hey cutie what you doin?

Amina: *Chilling in the bath tub. What you doin?*
Melody: *Trying to find something to get into.*
Amina: *Hmmm something like what?*
Melody: *You.*
Amina: *What's your address?*

I hope she can eat pussy good, I thought as I lathered my body with my tone coconut body wash.

Once I was out of the tub, I put on my coconut body oil, threw on a sundress, and dipped.

Amir kept calling me but I really didn't have much to say to him so I ignored his calls. He had too much drama going on at the moment for me.

Shit, I forgot to tell my mom I was leaving, I thought as I pulled up in front of Melody's house.

I didn't even have to knock on the door. Melody was standing in the door with nothing but some heels on.

Damn, I said to myself.

"Is that how you greet all of your company?" I asked.

"You like what you see?" she asked.

Instead of using words to show my appreciation, I fell to my knees and French kissed her lower lips.

"Mmmmm shiiittttt right there," she moaned.

I was tongue fucking her and rubbing her clit with my thumb at the same time.

"*Aahhhhh, I'm 'bout to cummmm. Shit I'm cummming,*" she screamed.

Her juices gushed out and I swallowed every drop of her sweetness.

Leaning against the door, spent from the powerful orgasm, Melody whispered, "Damn I don't even know your name." She laughed.

"Jade," I laughed.

"Well, Jade, let's go upstairs and get you out of that dress," she said.

I followed her to her room, which was decorated with candles.

As I was taking in the ambience, she walked up behind me placing kisses on my neck as she slid my dress to the floor.

Slowly walking me to the bed, she laid me down and mounted me.

She slowly started grinding against my pussy and playing with my nipples at the same time.

"Oooohhh," I moaned as I grabbed her hips.

She leaned forward and started sucking on my breast, right then left, paying them equal amounts of attention.

I was imagining Amir's lips kissing me as I felt myself reaching my peak.

I arched my back and gripped her hips tighter as I moaned, *"Fuckkkkk, right there, right there, shitttt,"* I moaned.

My body shook violently as my pussy creamed wetting both our stomachs and thighs.

Before I could catch my breath, Melody had her face in my pussy, sucking on my clit.

I bucked my hips as I ground my pussy against her tongue. She was working her tongue with expert skill. I was on the verge of another orgasm. Before I could let loose, she flipped me over and made me ride her face.

"Aaaaahhh shit, eat this pussy, bitch, eat this pussy," I moaned.

As I bounced and bucked on her tongue, I moaned, *"I'm cumming. Shitttttt, I'm cumming."*

I gushed all over her face. I collapsed beside her trying to catch my breath.

"Damn, Mel, I needed that," I breathlessly spoke.

"I love the way you taste," she giggled.

"You don't taste too bad yourself. Where's the bathroom?" I said as I got up and grabbed my dress.

By the time I was done washing myself up, Melody was sleep. I left her a note and headed home.

I wonder what Amir is doing, I said to myself.

It was 3 o'clock in the morning and I was hungry so I decided to stop at Waffle House to get something to eat.

I walked into the restaurant and took a seat the bar. I already knew what I wanted so I placed my order.

Once I got my food, I turned to leave and there stood Amir with none other than Keta.

"You better watch it, bitch," Keta smirked.

"No, bitch, *you* better watch it," I sneered.

Amir looked like a deer caught in headlights. I played it cool, walked up to him, and whispered, "This is why you'll never be more than a crush."

I patted his shoulder and walked out.

I lost my appetite so once I got home I put the food in the fridge for my mom.

When I finally fell asleep, the sun was coming up.

Phoenix

Chapter 4

I woke up Sunday feeling refreshed. I wasn't about to let anything get me down.

"Good afternoon, sleepy head," my mom said.

"Hey, lady," I said as I gave her a hug and kiss.

"Thanks for the food. I haven't had Waffle House in forever," she giggled.

The phone started ringing. I saw that it was Aunt Carol so I mouthed, "You're welcome."

Those two would be on the phone for hours so I went to my room to look over my notes for my exams tomorrow.

After about two hours of studying, I took a break and checked my phone. I had a few text messages and some missed calls. I only planned on returning two calls, Nique's and Farrah's.

"Hey, bookworm. What's up?" Nique giggled

"Hey, nothing, girl, taking a break from studying. What you doing?" I asked.

"Nothing, just finished doing Farrah's hair. We tried to call you to see if you wanted to come chill for a little bit," Nique said.

"Girl, y'all know I study on Sunday so I am staying in the house today," I said.

"Your ass is going to turn into a book," Farrah yelled in the background.

"Shut up. What y'all doing today?" I laughed.

"Girl, this hot box over here is trying to go to Oasis. You should come to," said Nique.

"I will think about it but I doubt if I go because I have school in the morning," I said.

"Well if you change your mind, let me know. I am about to go butter my man up." She ended the call.

I flopped down on my bed and fell asleep thinking of Amir.

***

Time seemed to drag by. Before I knew it, three weeks had passed.

Amir called everyday but I wasn't dealing with him until he got things straight on his end.

One day after school, while I was sitting at the bus stop, Nique and Amir pulled up.

Nique claimed she needed my help to find something to wear for a special date with Cas.

"I shouldn't have to use my cousin to get to you," Amir said from the backseat, looking like he lost his best friend.

I was giving Nique the "yea right" look as I questioned her about this special date. I must admit the, girl is good because my ass ended up in the car.

I knew it was bullshit but I never pass up a trip to the mall, so I threw my book bag in the back and hopped in the front seat.

To my surprise, Amir stayed with us the whole time.

Nique suddenly got a call about an emergency at the shop, which I knew was bullshit because Kema keeps everything in line when Nique isn't around, but I played along because I really missed Amir.

Once we dropped her off at the shop, the rest of the ride was awkwardly silent.

"Can you drop me off please?" I asked.

"Yea, after I handle this business," he said.

I rolled my eyes and exhaled harshly. *I knew I shouldn't have got my ass in this car. Damn, he looks good,* I thought as I stole glances at him.

We arrived at the Marriott and my first thought was *I know this nigga don't think he gettin' none cause he about to be in for a rude awakening.* He gave the car keys to the valet. We walked into the hotel restaurant. The hostess escorted us to a secluded booth that was set up for a romantic dinner.

He let me slide in, then he slid in next to me.

He turned to face me as he took my hands into his. He looked into my eyes and said, "Amina, I apologize. Keta, my ex, won't let go. I have told her numerous times that it will never be anything more than sex," he sincerely stated.

"Amir, I accept your apology. But until you can come correct, *we* will never be more than this," I said.

"All I'm asking for is a chance. I respect what you're saying..." He was saying but was cut off when the waiter came to our table with some appetizers and wine.

Once the waiter left, Amir continued talking, "I don't usually do this. You got a nigga open off one date."

"I have been open off you for a little minute, but I am not to be toyed with. We can see where this goes," I said as I took a bite of a breadstick.

Once all of that was out of the way, things flowed smoothly.

"So, *Bookworm,* since no man has ever tasted, touched, or seen your goodies, does that mean women have?" Amir asked with a smirk on his face.

Blushing, I answered, "Maybe, maybe not. A lady *never* kisses and tells."

"I like that in you. I am sure I will find out soon enough. I must say that I think it is sexy," he said.

"I bet you do," I said.

"You are an interestingly intriguing young lady. You have such a good girl vibe about you, *Bookworm,*" he said.

"I am going to kill Nique. I am a very good girl with bad girl tendencies, *sometimes,*" I flirted.

The waiter brought a dessert cart out with an assortment of fruits, dips, pies, and cakes on it. He chose a piece of chocolate mousse pie for us to share.

"Could you leave the cart and not disturb us for the next hour please?" Amir politely asked the waiter.

"Yes sir, if you need anything just come and find and me," said the waiter.

After the waiter disappeared, Amir turned to me and fed me a piece of pie.

I seductively ate the pie off the fork. My heart was beating in my ears. My thong was soaking wet. *Lord, I think I am falling in love,* I thought as I took my fork and returned the favor.

"You know you're goin' to be mine, right?" Amir said as he looked into my eyes and fed me another piece of pie.

"Mmmm, am I?" I asked, accepting the pie.

"You already are for real you're just scared to admit it," He stated confidently as he leaned in and licked some whip cream off my lips.

"Mmmm, if you say so," I said in between kisses.

He worked his way down to my neck as his hands found their way under my dress.

"*Damn,* baby girl," he moaned against my neck.

I was speechless. His fingers were working magic on my clit.

"*Amirrrr,*" I quietly moaned.

"Talk to me, baby girl," Amir whispered in my ear as he slowed down the pace.

"*Ohhh Amirrr,*" I moaned as I gripped the table.

"Talk to me, baby girl," He whispered again, and then kissed my neck and picked up the pace.

"*Fuckkkk, Amir, Amir, Amirrr,*" I moaned loudly as I began to grind my hips against his fingers.

Amir took his free hand and dipped it in chocolate first, then whip cream before he placed them in my mouth.

I grabbed his wrist. I looked him in the eyes as I slowly licked his fingers before I placed them in my mouth.

"*Mmmmm,*" I moaned as I sucked on his fingers.

I felt like I had to pee. *This is a feeling I never felt before,* I thought as I moved my hips faster.

"*Amirrrr Amirr, ooohhh, what are you doing to me? Shittt, I'm cumming,*" I moaned loudly as I released all over his fingers.

"Yea, *you're mine,*" said Amir as he licked his finger. "I'm keeping these, by the way," he said as he took my thong and put it in his pocket.

I was too spent to say anything. I just sat back and tried to catch my breath, thinking *damn.*

"Did you need anything else?" asked the waiter.

"No, just the check, please," Amir said.

As soon as the waiter was gone, he turned to me and asked, "Are you alright, baby girl."

Still unable to speak, I just nodded my head *yes* and took a drink of water.

Finally finding my voice, I asked, "Amir, could you let me out so that I can go to the ladies room, please? Amir, what did you do to me?" I shrieked as I fell back into the booth, realizing my legs were weak.

He just looked at me with a cocky smirk as he helped me out of the booth.

I slowly walked to the bathroom.

When I got into the restroom, I went straight into a stall and got myself together.

After I washed my hands, I stood there staring at my reflection and trying to figure out if I was really ready for Amir.

When I came out of the restroom, I found Amir standing there waiting for me.

"I didn't know if you would make it back to the table, so I came to carry you," he laughed.

"Shut up," I laughed as I punched him in the arm.

He held my hand as he drove me home. When we pulled up in front of my house he walked me to my door and kissed me goodnight.

After that dinner, we were inseparable. When I wasn't with him, we were on the phone talking or texting.

Chapter 5

Here it is a year later and Amir and I are still going strong.

"Girl remember when you used to do hair out of the house and I was your receptionist? Your mama used to cuss us out every day," I laughed.

"Cuss us out, then be like 'Mina, pencil me in for tonight.' Girl, you had the front porch setup like a waiting room for real, magazines and all," she laughed.

"Look at you now, you have *your* own shop and you're engaged," I said as I stood in the middle of *Beautifully Yours*.

"And for now, you're still my receptionist. The best one I ever had," Nique said as she put her arm around my shoulder.

I put my arm around hers and we just stood there taking it all in.

I turned to look at her as I placed my hands on her hips.

I was about to lean in for a kiss when Farrah burst through the doors louder than ever.

"What's up, ladies? Nique, can you tighten me up real quick?" Farrah asked as she sat down in Nique's chair.

"Do I have a choice?" Nique laughed as she walked over to her station.

"Not really. You know you're my hair genie," Farrah said.

Damn, her timing is always off. I wanted some of that wicked mouth she has. It has been a minute since I tasted my first, I thought as I watched Nique.

She licked her lips slowly causing a puddle to form in my panties.

I had been trying to fight these urges but I couldn't help it.

Amir might get lucky tonight. I have held out long enough, I thought as I took a seat.

"Bookworm, what's on your mind?" Farrah asked.

"It's not what, honey, it's *who,*" Nique said.

"Whatever, I am not thinking about Amir," I blushed.

"Look at her face," Farrah said to Nique while laughing.

"Seriously, I think I'm ready," I said.

"Ready for what?" they said in unison.

"Sex," I said.

"*Girl, you been holding out all this time. Why?*" They asked simultaneously.

"Okay, this creepy twin thing y'all have going on is freaking me out," I said while laughing. "I wanted to be sure he was the one. We have oral sex but no penetration," I explained.

"Girl, I woulda threw that pussy on him a long time ago. You know he fucking somebody, right?" Farrah stated confidently.

"Who won't you throw it on? Don't listen to her. I think it is romantic, but where and when did you learn to suck dick?" Nique questioned.

"Just know that I make my man's toes curl. I know he isn't fully satisfied tho," I somberly stated.

"Girl, don't pay me no mind. Amir would *never* cheat on you," Farrah said.

"When I finish her, we are going to go to the mall and get you together," Nique said.

I put my ear buds in and thought to myself *Amir wouldn't cheat on me, would he?*

Farrah
Mina doesn't know how to handle a man like Amir. She should

have stuck with those bitches she been licking and sucking on. I am surprised she's still a virgin. Look at her over there looking pitiful because she's scared of the dick. I am so sick of her. All our life it has always been about little Miss Amina. Farrah, you should be like Amina. Look at what Amina did Farrah. I am so proud of her, I thought as Nique curled my hair.

What the fuck is so special about her anyway?

"Earth to Farrah," Nique said as she waved her hand in front of my face.

"I'm sorry, what were you saying?" I asked.

"Girl, I am done with your hair. Are you going to the mall with us?" Nique asked.

"Naw, I am going to head home and relax before I go to work. Come make it rain on me when y'all done running around. Bookworm, I hope you didn't take what I said to heart. Mir ain't crazy. I love y'all," I said as I walked out of the shop.

Thank god that is finally over, I said to myself as I hopped in my cocaine white Benz.

Amina

"Pick ya face up. Girl, you know Farrah don't know what she talking about," Nique said.

"I'm good. Let's go tear the mall up," I said as I grabbed my purse and walked towards the door behind Nique.

My phone went off, alerting me that I had a message. I pulled my phone out to check it. It was from Amir.

Amir: *Baby girl pack a bag, I have a surprise for you.*

Amina: *Give me a hint.*

Amir: *Nope. Just be ready by 11.*

Amina: :-(*Ok baby. I'm bout to go to the mall with Ni. Ttyl*

Amir: *Do you need any money?*

Amina: *No baby.*

I ended the conversation and put my phone back in my bag.

When we arrived at the mall, Nique took me straight to the sex store, G-Spot.

"Okay Bookworm, let's get you together," she excitedly said more to herself than to me.

She walked thru the store grabbing an assortment of things, which I don't think were all for me. I was strolling alongside her looking at some of the different toys when a double ended dildo caught my eye.

Smiling, I held the toy up and asked, "Nique, want to try this?"

"Girl, get your cherry popped first." She laughed but I saw the lust in her eyes.

I held on to the toy and we continued shopping.

Finally, we got to the lingerie section.

"Since you're a virgin, let's get you something lacy and white," she said.

We both were going from rack to rack until I excitedly yelled, "I found it. This is the one. What do you think?"

I held up a lace white one piece. The top was made like a bustier but it was all lace and the bottom half was made like boy shorts.

"Oh, my Bookworm is growing up. He is going to love you in that," Nique said.

"You think so?" I asked as I blushed.

"I know so," she said.

We went to check out and then we hit a couple more stores before we left the mall.

"Where are we going to eat?" I asked.

"I'm not really hungry. Are you going to Clappers?" Nique asked.

"No, Mir told me to be ready at 11pm because he had a surprise for me," I said.

"Oh okay well have fun and fill me in when you can. I won't worry because I know you're good hands," Nique said.

It was an unusually warm night in April. Since I had some time to kill, I sat and chilled with my mom.

"Hey, pumpkin, I am surprised you're home. Where's your boyfriend at?" asked my mom.

"Gosh, don't say it like that, mom. He will be to get me at 11 tho," I said as I playfully bumped her.

"I'm just saying I never get to see you between school, the shop, and my job," my mom said, sounding kind of down.

"Hey, lady, don't sound so down. Since I am on spring break, I will be home a little more," I said.

"Child please, I ain't down at all. I love having the house to myself. What time is my son-in-law picking you up anyway?" she asked while cracking up laughing.

Feigning like I was hurt, I placed my hand over my chest.

"He will be here in the next thirty minutes. Why are you so ready for me to leave?" I asked while smiling.

"What are y'all doing tonight?" she asked.

"He wouldn't tell me. He just told me to pack a bag," I said.

"Oh okay," said my mom.

I felt like she knew something I didn't know and there was no use in trying to get it out of her.

"Well, I am going to make sure I have everything. Let me know when he gets here," I said as I got up to leave.

"I seen that G-Spot bag. All I am going to say is be safe. You have your whole life ahead of you. If it don't feel right, *don't* do it," she said.

I walked into the house in complete shock and a little embarrassed.

My momma don't miss a beat. What she know about G-spot? I asked myself.

I made sure I had everything then I grabbed my phone and texted Nique.

Amina: *It's been too long. I know you miss me.*

Nique: *It has and I do.*

Amina: *Had Farrah not showed up, we would have christened the shop.*

Nique: *I know, her timing has always been a little off. Lol*

Amina: *Tell me about it, lol. I am getting that soon. ;-P*

Nique: *What if I don't give it to you?*

Amina: *I have ways of getting it.*

"Mina, Mir's here," yelled my mom.

"Okay, here I come," I said.

Amina: *My boo is here but don't think this convo is over. Ttyl*

After I sent that last text, I powered my phone down.

I grabbed my bag and went downstairs.

"Hey, baby," I said as I wrapped my arms around Amir.

"Y'all be safe. Mina, remember what I told you," said my mom as she hugged me.

"Alright, Ms. Trina, see you later," Amir said as he hugged my mom.

Once we were in the car, he kissed me passionately.

"Are you going to tell me where we are going?" I asked.

"No, baby girl. It is a surprise. We have a long ride ahead of us."

"Baby, that's not fair," I pouted.

"You're cute when you pout," he smirked.

"Tell me, baby," I said as I batted my lashes.

"That isn't going to work, bookworm. Baby, you're going to like this surprise," he said.

"*Okay, baby,*" I said then I leaned over and kissed his cheek.

"Mina, don't start nothing," he said as he caressed my thigh.

"*Don't* you start," I giggled.

It wasn't really much to see at night, so I got comfortable and went to sleep.

Phoenix

Chapter 6

Amir

I hated riding with so much work on me. I could have had one of my workers make the run, but it wasn't just a work trip. It was our one year anniversary. *This girl got me doing things I never done. Am I in love?* I asked myself.

I'd never had to wait a year to get no pussy. *I must be in love. I would give this girl the world if I could. She is so beautiful, so innocent. I know she's what I need,* I thought.

I hoped Kandi was ready when I got there because I was ready to be balls deep in some pussy. I stopped fucking Keta because she was becoming a headache. All she had to do was be cool and she still would have been getting the dick. That was one of the reasons why we didn't last, she was always on that drama shit. Now, Kandi, I had been fucking with her sexy chocolate ass for the past six months. She knew it was just sex and she was cool with that.

I know I'm wrong but I have needs. I am not going to pressure her. When she's ready, she'll let me know. My baby head game is official but I need more than just my dick sucked. When we start fucking, I'll stop cheating, I thought to myself as I glanced at her.

After driving four hours straight, we are finally there.

I hate to wake her. She looks so peaceful, I thought as I watched her sleep for a lil bit.

Amina

"Baby girl, wake up. We're here," he said as he slightly shook me.

37

Phoenix

I stretched as I opened my eyes taking in the scenery.

Mardis Gras Casino and Resort, I said to myself as I stepped out of the car.

I didn't know where we were but I knew we weren't in Tribeca anymore.

"Come on, baby girl, I know you're ready to shower and crash," Amir said as he helped me out of the car.

It's 3 in the morning, wonder who he's calling, must be business, I thought as I watched Amir walk out onto the balcony to make a call. I shrugged it off and went to take a hot shower.

***

"Kandi, what room are you in?" Amir asked.

"2032, my pussy is ready for you, daddy," Kandi said.

"Did you leave a key for me at the desk like I told?" he asked.

"Yes daddy," Kandi said.

"Let me hear it. You know we getting straight to it when I get there," Amir stated.

"*Mmmmm hmmm,*" Kandi moaned as she fingered herself.

"*Damn,* I can't wait to get that," Amir stated as he heard the balcony door open.

Amina

Feeling freaky after my shower, I walked out on the balcony and unzipped Amir's pants, freeing his dick while he was on the phone.

I licked around the head teasingly before I deep throated his dick, which caused him to lose focus on the phone. *I hope it wasn't business,* I thought as I continued to deep throat his cock.

38

"*Shittt,* baby girl, do that shit," Amir moaned.

I was slurping, slobbing, and moaning on his tool as I worked my hand up, down, and around his member.

"*Fuck,*" Amir exclaimed as he gripped the phone tighter with one hand and gripped my hair with the other.

"You like that, daddy? Mmmmm," Kandi moaned.

"*Aaaaahhh fuck,* baby, do that shit," Amir moaned.

I took his penis deep into my mouth and hummed on the mushroom tip of it. I knew he was about to cum because I felt his body tense up.

"*Fuck,* get that nut, baby," Amir said as he released his load in my mouth.

I looked up at him as I swallowed all his cum.

He slowly slid his member out of my mouth as he leaned up against the balcony door trying to catch his breath.

Amir

Fuck, I hope Kandi is ready. That fire head got me ready to tear something up, I thought as I pulled out my phone.

I looked down to see that Kandi was trying to call me. I couldn't answer because Mina was laying up under a nigga.

Damn, I thought as I looked at the way her ass looked in the lace black boy shorts.

Yea, I'm 'bout to get ghost 'cause I need to be in something wet, I thought as I watched her begin to fall asleep.

"Baby, I gotta go handle some business. Let's get you in the bed," I said as I carried her to the bed.

"Okay," Mina mumbled against my neck.

I laid her down gently. Then I dipped out to get the room key for Kandi's room.

My tool was ready to put in work, so I let myself in her room.

When I walked in, Kandi was spread eagle in the middle of the bed.

"Make that pussy squirt for me," I said as I stood at the foot of the bed.

She rubbed her love button with lightning speed, which caused her to scream out, "*Ohhh shit, Amir, daddy, daddy,*" moaned Kandi as she squirted.

Turned on by the sight, I dove in head first before she could recover.

I sucked on her sensitive clit gently as I worked two fingers in and out of her juice box.

"*Ahhh shit, Mir,*" she moaned.

I released her clit and started tongue fucking her slowly, gradually picking up the pace.

"Cum for me," I said against her clit.

"*Amir, Amir, oh shit I'm cumming. I'm cumming. Oh god I'm cumming,*" Kandi screamed out as she showered me with her love.

As soon as she caught her breath, I sensually kissed and slowly slid my stiff tool inside her.

"Amir, don't stop. *Please* don't stop," Kandi moaned.

I put her legs in the bend of my arms and started stroking her deep and hard.

"*Damn, shit,* baby, squeeze my dick," I lowly moaned.

"*Right there, right there. Oh shit, Mir, I'm cumming. Fuck, I'm cumming.*" Kandi moaned as she dug her nails deep into my back.

As I flipped her on top of me, she eased down on my dick slowly and began to ride.

I gripped her hips as I lifted up to put my tool all the way in, taking her breath away.

"*Daddyyy*," Kandi yelped as I dug deeper.

She matched my stroke forcefully, trying to regain control, so I gave in and let her have it. She bounced up and down on my dick slow then fast.

"*Fuck. Ride this dick. Ride this dick.*" I said aggressively as I thrust my hips upwards a few times.

"*Ami... shit.*" She moaned loudly as she sat down on my dick rocking her hips.

I felt my balls tighten. I couldn't hold back anymore so I flipped her over and pounded away.

"Don't run. Take this dick. *Take this dick,*" I exclaimed as I pulled her hair.

The sight of her ass rippling after each stroke made me go harder. I loved seeing that shit.

Thank god Mina has a phat ass, I thought as I coated her walls.

"Shit girl you trying to make sure a nigga never let you go, huh?" I asked as I tapped her on her ass and collapsed on the bed.

"I'm wifey for real. *You* just scared to admit it," Kandi stated confidently.

I didn't bother responding to the delusional shit she was talking.

Mina is wifey. You just a cum disposal to me, I thought as I drifted off to sleep.

Damn, I love the way she gives me head. I wish she would gon' head and let me pop her cherry, I thought as I felt a warm mouth on my dick.

"*Fuck,* baby, keep doing that shit," I moaned as I placed my hand on her head.

What the... how the... fuck. Mina is going to kill me. Damn, she is working that mouth tho, I thought as I looked down into Kandi's eyes. She was making my shit disappear with ease. I got so mad at myself for enjoying it but I wasn't going to stop her. I couldn't stop her. It was feeling too damn good.

I started moving my legs to the edge of the bed so that I could get up, thinking she would release the hold she had on my dick. But she didn't.

Moving with me, she kept up her pace, never missing a beat.

Her amazing head skills were what kept me coming back. Don't get me wrong, the pussy was good, but I loved the way she sucked my dick.

Fuck, I gotta stop, I thought as I started to aggressively fuck her mouth.

I was mad at her for sucking me so damn good.

I was mad at myself for enjoying it.

"*Shit. Suck. That. Dick, bitch. Just. Like. That,*" I exclaimed with each thrust.

My toes were curling. *Damn,* I thought as I pumped harder as my tool erupted like a volcano.

I squirted cum all over her face, cleaned my tool off, and left.

Once I was in the hall, I looked back at the door tempted to go back.

I can't go back. I gotta stop doing this to Mina. Damn, what's a young nigga to do? I thought as I placed my hand on the door.

Instead of going straight up to the room, I decided to go for a ride and clear my mind.

I was just riding through the city, taking in the sights, watching the city come alive.

What the fuck am I doing with Mina? She has more class than most of the women I encounter. She's a good girl. I don't want to corrupt her. I have never cared about a bitch, but I don't want to hurt her. Damn a nigga losing his playa ways, I chuckled to myself as I pulled up at a local florist shop.

"I am done fucking wit Kandi," I said as I walked in the door.

"Good morning, Sir, how may I help you?" said the florist.

"Good morning, may I get two dozen red roses with a card that says *Happy Anniversary*," I asked.

"Could you have them delivered to Mardi Gras Hotel suite 1732? Also, could you send a dozen pink roses to the same hotel suite 2032? Thank you," I said.

"That will be three hundred dollars," the florist said.

I gave her my credit card and left.

By the time I got to the hotel, it was 8 o'clock in the morning.

Mina must still be sleep. She hasn't called or texted. This just might work in my favor, I thought as I entered the room.

I took off my clothes and quietly slid in the bed. I didn't put my arms around her because I didn't want her to wake up.

I must've been sleep for about fifteen minutes when I felt her attempting to get out of the bed.

"Where you going?" I asked as I wrapped my arms around her waist, pulling her in to me.

"Baby, let me go. I gotta use the bathroom," she giggled.

I tickled her a little bit. Then I loosened my hold on her and she took off running.

I laughed to myself as I lay back on the bed. There was a knock at the door.

"Baby girl, come get the door," I yelled from the bed.

"Why can't you get it?" she asked.

"Okay, baby girl, don't get mad if it's a chick and she fall down on her knees to bless me 'cause you got me answering the door naked and shit," I said as I pretended to get out of the bed.

"Mir, please don't make me hurt you and the bitch at the door," she said glaring at me as she walked to the door.

I knew who was at the door. I just laid there waiting for her reaction.

"Thank you, baby," Mina said as she dropped to her knees and took my tool into her warm mouth.

Amina

The roses were beautiful so I decided to properly thank him. I walked back into the room and dropped to my knees.

"Happy anniversary, daddy," I said as I took his tool into my mouth until I felt the head at the back of my throat.

"Hmmm. Mmmmm. Hmmm," I hummed on his love stick as my hand twisted and turned up and down his tool.

I am going to make tonight real special, I thought as I picked up the pace.

I took his balls into my mouth one by one, then both at the same time while humming on them and stroking his dick.

I used my free hand to play with my pussy as continued to pleasure him.

"Mina, I'm 'bout to cum, baby. Get this nut, baby," Amir moaned as he thrust his hips.

I loved the taste of him, so I put my mouth back on his tool and worked my magic mouth until I got my reward.

"Shit, I'm cumming," Amir said as he sprayed my throat with his seeds.

"Thanks for breakfast, daddy," I said as I got up off my knees and went to the bathroom to get ready for the day.

"Baby, I will be back in thirty minutes. Meet me in the lobby in thirty minutes, baby. I love you," I yelled through the bathroom door.

I know I said I was done with Kandi but I need to get this nut out of me, I thought as I grabbed my things to leave.

I walked into Kandi's room. She was sleeping peacefully.

I took my clothes off as I approached the bed slowly stroking my semi-erect dick. I pulled the covers back and slid my tool deep inside her tightness.

"Damn," I moaned in her ear as placed kisses all over her neck and back.

She slightly lifted her ass and started throwing it back on my tool.

"Fuck me harder, Mir. Oh Mir, I love you," Kandi moaned loudly as threw her ass back harder.

"Throw. That. Ass. Back," I said as I thrust my dick deep inside of her hard and fast.

I knew this shit had to end, I grabbed a handful of hair and fucked her until I busted all over her back.

We hopped in the shower together. Then I left to meet my girl.

I made it down to the lobby in time to see Mina step off the elevator.

"Hey, baby. You look amazing," I said as I gave her a quick kiss on the lips.

"Thank you, baby," Mina said as she looped her arm in mine.

I decided that we would be tourists today, so we went on a walk around the city, just taking in the sites and shopping.

Just before sunset, I surprised her with a carriage ride.

Amina

"Baby this is so romantic," I exclaimed as we watched the sunset.

"It's our anniversary, it's our anniversary, baby," he started singing to me while looking in my eyes.

I was speechless. I didn't know he could sing. I was so lost in his eyes and the moment that I didn't realize we had stopped.

We were back at the hotel, where we were escorted to the French Quarter restaurant.

I was in awe of the décor. I felt like I was in France. We were seated in an area that was made to look as if we were on a balcony with a view of the Eiffel Tower.

He is definitely getting some tonight. I may have to send him to gamble for a while so that I can prepare myself, I thought as I gazed into his honey colored eyes.

I was just about to kiss him when his phone started ringing. I wasn't upset that he took the call because this may be just the distraction I need and I really wasn't that hungry.

"Baby, you wouldn't be mad if I had to cut dinner short, would you?" Amir asked.

"No, baby, I wasn't really that hungry anyway," I said.

"I will make it up to you, baby," Amir said. Then he gave me a quick kiss.

"How long will you be gone?" I asked.

"An hour or two, I shouldn't be that long tho," he said as he walked me to the elevator.

"I will be waiting up for you. Be careful, Mir," I said as I got in the elevator.

Since I had some time to kill, I called Nique to get some advice.

"Hey, girl, how is everything going?" Nique asked.

"Well hello to you, too. Girl, it has been amazing," I exclaimed.

"Wait a minute, why are you on the phone?" she asked.

"He got called away for an emergency. I am going to give him the cookie tonight," I said.

"*Shut up,*" Nique screeched while laughing.

"Yes, so I need some tips to set the mood," I giggled.

"Get some candles, chocolate, fruit, and wine. Make it like a romantic scavenger hunt. You will be the prize at the end," she said.

"He will be so surprised. Girl, let me get off of here so I can go get the stuff and set up. I will call you later," I said, then ended the call.

I rushed out of the room with excitement.

I went to the supermarket and bought all of the things Nique recommended and then some.

Phoenix

Chapter 7

Amir

This nigga Havoc's timing is amazing. Shit, Hav and I go way back. Hav is part of the reason I am who I am today. Damn here she go again. Kandi been blowing my phone up, I know Mina felt it vibrating. My girl don't trip about much, I haven't really given her a reason. I am goin to end it as soon as get back to the hotel. I am going to send her home, I thought as I pulled up to Havoc's house.

"Havoc, what's good, nigga?" I said.

"Shit trying to get this money so I can be like you one day," Havoc said as he gave me dap.

"*Shit,* I'm trying to get like you," I said as I lit a blunt and took a pull on it. Then I passed it to him.

"I know you were chilling with your lady but we down to our last and I can't have lil niggas out here with idle hands, ya feel me?" Havoc said as he took a couple pulls on the blunt and passed it back.

"My lady ain't tripping. Nigga, I'm low key glad you called. Yea, idle hands lead to dumb shit happening fo sho," I said as I inhaled the exotic herbs and held it in.

"You got a good one then 'cause I can't get my girl to shut up. Her ass stay yapping 'bout nothing," he said.

"Yea, but shit is getting old ya know. She still holding out on a nigga. I mean I'm getting satisfied elsewhere but I want that in house, feel me?" I said.

"Damn, nigga, you been with her for a hot little minute and you still ain't hit? I don't see how you doing it, bruh," he exclaimed while shaking his head laughing.

"*Nigga*, I flew Kandi out here. I refuse to pressure her. She will let me know when she's ready to take things to that level. Shit, a nigga has needs tho, feel me?" I said as I put what was left of the blunt out.

"Yea, I feel you for sure, been there done that. Now I can't rid of her ass," Havoc laughed.

"Nigga, you love her and you ain't goin' nowhere. How is Faith anyway?" I said while laughing.

"I'm not trying to. Faith got a nigga forever. Other than driving me crazy, she good. We should all hook up before you go back home," Havoc said.

"That sounds like a plan. Well, I am about to get back to my girl and see what the rest of the night has in store. A nigga might get lucky," I said with a slight laugh as I gave him a man hug.

"A'ight, man, thanks for coming thru early," he said.

"You're welcome," I said as I got in my car and rode off.

When I pulled up to the hotel, it was 11 o'clock, so I decided to go holla at Kandi. I gave the valet my keys and went straight to Kandi's room.

"Kandi, come out here so we can talk," I said as I walked in and sat on the couch.

"*Kandi,*" I yelled with more bass in my voice.

I know her ass was trying to get me to come in the room, but I wasn't falling for that trick.

"Stop with the fucking games. *Come here, now,*" I said as I went over to the bar to make a drink.

"Yes, how may I help you?" Kandi said as she stood in the middle of the living room with nothing but some red heels on.

Damn, focus nigga, focus, I thought to myself as I watched her standing there oiled up looking good enough to eat. I gulped my drink down in one swallow.

"Pack your bags, your flight leaves at 2am," I said assertively.

"*You* pack 'em. Why are you sending me home, Mir?" she stated with her hands on her hips.

"This shit has got to stop. I'm here with my girl," I said.

"And that means what to me? You know you don't mean that. Come here, daddy," Kandi said as she walked towards me.

"I am *serious,* it's over," I said as I tried to move away from the bar.

I should have just sent a text or something. She making this shit hard, I thought to myself as she moved closer.

"I'm out," I said as I started walking to the door.

"Okay, let me suck your dick one last time," Kandi said standing in front the door.

I tried to move her out of the way, but she would not budge.

Looking me in my eyes as she unzipped my pants, She slid down into a squatting position. She released my snake and began to charm it. Never taking her eyes off of mine, she took my tool deep into the depths of her mouth.

Fuck, I need to stop her. Damn, this feels so good. This is the last time. Fuck, this is the last time, I thought as I watched my dick disappear into her mouth.

My mind was telling me to stop her but it was feeling too good. I grabbed a handful of her hair and began to slowly make love to her mouth.

Hearing her slightly gag on my tool and continue to slurp and moan on my dick turned me on even more. I picked up the pace.

Thrusting my hips back and forth, I watched my tool disappear over and over again.

Since this is the last time, I might as well go in, I thought as I grabbed a handful of her hair.

"*Fuck. Fuck. Fuck.*" I yelled as I came down her throat.

"Bend that ass over," I stated.

I put my dick deep inside of her in one swift motion, causing her to scream out.

"*Mir. Oh Mir. Fuck me,*" Kandi moaned loudly.

"Throw that ass back. Throw. It. Back. Bitch." I stated aggressively as I pulled her hair and fucked her harder.

"*Yasss, Amir, yassss. Oh my god, I love you,*" Kandi screamed out.

"Work that shit," I stated as I let her hair go and stood there watching her bounce all over my tool.

I felt myself about to cum so I gripped her hips and went hard.

"*Aaahhhh shit,*" I exclaimed as I nutted deep inside of her.

I pulled my dick out of her and then I went to the bathroom to clean myself up.

What the fuck did I just do, I asked myself as I realized that I just came in her.

"Come on so I can walk you out," I said holding the door open.

"Damn, I don't need you to escort me out. *I'm leaving, daddy,*" Kandi said with sass.

"I ain't worried about that. I just want to see you off, that's all, baby. We still cool. We just can't fuck no more," I said as we got on the elevator.

Once we reached the lobby, she touched my cheek softly and said, "I'm going to miss that dick. You hit spots that I never knew existed." She smiled up at me.

I just looked down at her with a smirk on my face.

"You are something, Chocolate," I said as the car pulled up in front. I walked her through the sliding doors.

"I will call when I get home." Kandi said. Then she reached up and kissed me sweetly as I palmed her ass.

Amina

I looked at the clock and it read 1:30 am. *Amir should be on his way back. I better hurry up and take this note downstairs,* I thought as I grabbed the envelope and walked out of the room.

I got off the elevator and was rendered speechless by what I saw.

My man, Amir, talking to some thick sexy chocolate chick.

Mina, calm down. It may just be business. See what happens before you go fuck him and her up, I told myself as I took several deep calming breaths.

I walked closer to the doors just enough to get a clear view of them, but not close enough that the doors would open.

Is he kissing this hoe? Naw, I gotta be seeing things. I'm not tripping this nigga just kissed her and palmed her ass. Oh hell naw. He has me fucked up, I thought as I walked out the doors to catch them before they left.

"Hi, you two make a lovely couple. *Happy* anniversary, Mr. Carter," I said as the tears welled up in my eyes.

"Mina, let me…" Amir tried to speak but I cut him off.

"Let you what? *Explain.* What you gon' say?" I ranted.

"Baby, she was just leaving," Amir yelled as the chocolate chick turned to get in the car.

"Please, sweetie, don't leave on my account. Amir, it's cool. You're just like the rest. I see that now. Y'all have a nice time," I said as I walked away.

Amir

What the fuck was I thinking? I asked myself as I watched her walk away.

"Kandi, thanks for not saying nothing. Let me know when you land," I said, and then walked away.

I didn't know what I was going to do but I knew I had to do something.

"Excuse me, may I speak with your manager please?" I asked the girl at the front desk.

"Yes, sir, just a moment," she said.

"Hi, I am Chelsea, the manager. Is everything okay?

"Chelsea, I am here with my girlfriend in suite 1732, for our one year anniversary and I am trying to surprise her."

"Not to overstep but I saw the exchange outside and you're trying to get out of the dog house, right?" she asked with a slight giggle.

"You seen that? You are right tho," I said.

"What would you like for us to do?" she asked.

"I would like to get a penthouse suite. I want to have roses placed throughout the room. I would also like some chocolate, whip cream, and fresh fruit placed in the bedroom buffet style.

"Okay, sir, I can help you with that. It may take some time but it can be done," she said cheerfully.

"Spare no expense," I said as I handed her my black card.

Amina

I was hurt I wanted to whoop his ass, and hers, but fuck it, it wasn't worth it.

I went back to the room to pack my bags.

I am glad I have my own money, I thought as I called down to the front desk.

The lady told me that it would be an hour before I was able to get a room.

I hope he doesn't bring his ass up here trying to talk. I know he has needs but he could have sat me down and we could have made an arrangement, I thought as I lay across the bed.

He came trying to get in but I wasn't opening the door for him. He finally got the picture after standing out there for fifteen minutes.

I didn't want to hear shit he had to say.

I planned on enjoying the rest of my time here and then catching the Greyhound home.

I must have fallen asleep because the next thing I knew, I was awakened by a knock on the door.

Ugh, if this is Amir's sorry ass, I am going to fucking scream, I thought as I went to answer the door.

"Sorry to disturb you, Ms. Reynolds. I am Chelsea, the front desk manager, but the room you reserved was mistakenly given to a couple who had a prior reservation. I'm sorry for the inconvenience. We have arranged for you to move to a suite, at no additional cost to you, for duration of your stay due to the error being on our end," the front desk manager informed me.

"Okay, let me grab my bags," I said as I grabbed my bags and followed the lady to the elevator.

Once we were on the elevator, she put her key card in and the elevator went straight to the penthouse level.

"Enjoy your stay, Ms. Reynolds," she said, and then she disappeared.

When I walked into the room, I was in awe. It was so beautiful and the view was amazing. I walked out on the balcony and enjoyed the night air, wishing I would have grabbed some of Mir's weed to smoke.

I was in deep thought, enjoying the view, when I heard, "Baby, I'm sorry. I don't want lose you. I know you aren't ready for sex and I didn't want you to feel pressured. I'm sorry, Amina. I love you, ma."

I still had my back turned to him.

He put his arms around my waist as he kissed my neck, telling me how much he loved me between each kiss.

He led me to the bathroom, where there was bubble bath waiting. We bathed, he washed my body and I washed his.

Once we got out of the tub, he carried me to the bed. He gently laid me down and gave me a full body massage. He kissed every spot that his hands touched. My body was on fire and he was the only one that could put it out. He kissed me passionately as he played with my pearl.

"Baby, are you sure this what you want?" Amir asked as he looked me in the eyes.

"Yes, baby," I sensually whispered.

Once I gave him the green light, he kissed my hairless mound. Slowly sucking on my clit, he started slow fucking me with his tongue.

My body started shaking, which caused him to lick faster. He worked his finger in and out of my wetness with fury.

I was on the verge of another climax when he stopped to put a condom on. He climbed on top of me and eased the head in. I gasped from the pain. A tear ran down my cheek and he kissed it away.

"Baby, I can stop if you want me to," he said.

I kissed him to let him know that it was okay to keep going.

He went deeper, finally getting all ten inches buried deep inside of me.

"I love you, Amir."

"I love you too, ma."

We made love until the sun came up.

The rest of the trip was fun. I didn't want to leave but I had to go to school.

Phoenix

Chapter 8

Once we got home, it seemed like time flew by. School was almost over. My eighteenth birthday was two weeks away.

Amir and I hadn't spent much time together since we came back from Virginia, but we talked daily. I didn't mind though because school and work kept me busy.

I had been working as the shampoo girl at *Beautifully Yours* for the past three years. Working at the shop had its ups and downs but that came with any job.

The day before my birthday, I was in the shop washing a client's hair and talking to her about my plans after high school when loud mouth Kela walked in. I was instantly irritated because she was always in there running her dick sucker. I tried my best to ignore her, but my interest was piqued when she mentioned my man's name.

As she told her story about him and Keta, she was watching my every move. According to Kela, Keta had recently given birth to his baby. Supposedly, he'd been by her side for the past two weeks.

I was getting hotter by the second, but I refused to let her see me upset. I remained calm, finished washing my client's head, and started working on the next client.

I guess she didn't like the reaction she was getting from me so she moved on to her next juicy piece of gossip.

Just as she changed the subject, in walked Amir's sexy ass. Now I could have put her loud mouth ass on blast, but I chose to handle this in a different way. I was not about to put my business in the streets.

I walked up to him and wrapped my arms around his neck,

which wasn't easy because my baby is six feet eight inches tall with an athletically slim build, honey colored eyes, and a low cut Caesar with waves that would make you sea sick.

He lifted me up to his level. I felt Kela watching our every move as we kissed.

When we finally came up for air, he whispered, "You think you slick, ma."

Of course I played dumb as I looked at him innocently.

"Baby, what are you talking 'bout? I just missed you a whole lot," I said.

"Yea, okay, we'll talk later 'cause I got some shit to tell you anyway. But first, close your eyes," he said.

I closed my eyes as he walked us out the door. When I opened my eyes, there was a '95 black on black Yukon parked with a big red ribbon on it.

I kissed him once more, and then hopped out of his arms to go check out my new ride.

"Well, baby, I'mma let you get back to work. I got some more business to take care of. Love you, ma," he said.

"Love you, too," I said as I walked back into the shop.

Just like that, he was gone and so was Kela.

Mission accomplished, I thought as I laughed to myself.

I locked up the shop and went to show Nique my new whip.

***

When I got to Nique's, Cas was outside talking to some guy with dreads.

He was sexy as hell but he had a sinister look about him, so I gave Cas a hug and went inside to find Nique. Their house was a mini mansion.

I knew where she would be, in her massive closet, looking for something to wear for her date.

Thursday night was date night for her and Cas.

Usually, they'd make a whole day of it.

I thought that was so cute. Anyway, when I found her, I started filling her in on the day's events.

"Tell me why Kela tired ass came in the shop talking 'bout Keta just had a baby. Guess who the daddy is supposedly?" I said as we walked downstairs.

"*Who?*" Nique asked as she made us a drink.

"Amir," I said, and then took a sip of my drink.

"Stop lying," laughed Nique.

"Girl, I am so serious. The whole time she was talking she was watching me. I kept my cool. I was not about to let her take me off my square," I said.

"I know you were ready to tear shit up. What is he saying?" Nique asked.

"I haven't asked him about it yet. I have something to show you," I said as I grabbed her hand and led her outside.

"Look what my baby got me," I stated excitedly.

"Look at you, bitch. This is nice," Nique said as she walked around the truck.

"Thank you. He surprised me at the shop. Girl, Kela ass was tuned in," I said.

"Fuck her, she need to find something to do other than run her mouth. Well, I am going to go in here and freshen up for my date. Call me tomorrow," Nique said as she hugged me.

"Have fun," I said as I got in my truck and rode off.

***

I was kind of tired, so I went home, took a hot shower, talked to my mom for a little bit, and then went to sleep.

I woke up at two o'clock in the morning, so I called Amir.

"Hey, baby, what are you doing up?" he greeted me when he answered the phone.

"What's good? Are you busy?" I said.

"Not for real. What's the matter?" he asked.

"So is the baby yours? Is that where you've been?" I asked angrily.

"Baby, I will be there in ten minutes," he said with a sigh.

He pulled up in exactly ten minutes. I kept my PJs on because this shit was about to be real short. I got in the car with an attitude.

"So?" I said with my arms folded across my chest.

"Baby, Keta did just have a baby. It isn't mine tho," Amir said.

Turning to face him, I asked, "So is that where you've been?"

He just stared out the window into the darkness.

"Amir, I know *you* hear me. Is that where you've been?" I asked more assertively.

"Baby girl," he said as he turned to look me in the eyes.

"Fuck that baby girl shit. Answer the damn question," I stated.

"Yes, Amina, I was with Keta, but..." he said.

"But what?" I yelled.

"I was only around 'cause I was waiting on the DNA results to come back. I wanted to be sure before I came to you with it," he stated as he lit a blunt that was in the ashtray.

"I shouldn't have to hear the shit from somebody else. It should have come from you," I said as I jabbed him in the side of the head.

"Mina, don't get fucked up," he gritted.

"Is that why you got me the truck?" I asked.

"No, that was an early graduation gift. I should have come to you with it. I'm sorry you had to hear about it elsewhere," he said.

"If this isn't what you want, let me know now," I said.

"I wouldn't be here if I didn't. I don't have time to waste so if you can't handle it, let me know *now*," he asserted.

I just sat there looking at him as if he had two heads.

Did this nigga really just say this fool ass shit? He must think he got it like that. I'm going to show his ass, I thought as I got out of the car, not bothering to look back.

Happy birthday, I said to myself as I walked in the house.

I went straight to my room and tried to get some sleep.

I woke up at 7am determined to have a good day. My mom and I had breakfast. Then I went to school.

It seemed like time was moving at a snail's pace. I couldn't wait to get out of school. I was ready to party.

When I got out of school, I went to the shop to get my hair, nails, and feet done. I went to the mall to get an outfit. When I got home, it was going on eight o'clock.

I was about to start getting ready when the phone rang.

"Hello," I greeted.

"Amina, you gotta come to the hospital," Nique said.

"What's going on?" I asked.

"It's bad, Mina. Just get here, please. We are at Tribeca General," Nique said.

"I'm on my way," I said, and then hung up the phone.

I put on some sweats, a t-shirt, and some maxes. Then I grabbed my keys and hurried out the door.

Phoenix

***

When I got to the hospital, Cas, Nique, and a few members of the crew were there. I knew it wasn't good.

"Where's Amir?" I asked.

"Mina, sit down," Nique said.

"Naw, I'm good. Where's Amir?" I asked more aggressively.

I saw the grim expression on her face and it scared me. "Nique, please tell me what happen," I asked.

"Cas and Mir were out handling business when some niggas opened fire on 'em. Mir was hit five times. He's in critical condition," Nique solemnly stated.

"Is he going to make it? Was Cas hit?" I asked.

"Cas was hit in the arm. Things are touch and go right now," Nique said.

It was as if the world stopped. I was numb as the tears fell from my eyes. For the first time in a long time, I prayed.

***

For two months, I existed without Amir. I went to school and work. I spent every night at the hospital. One morning, I decided not to go to school and I stayed by Amir's side.

"Call Cas and tell him to come get you so you can take your ass to school," Amir whispered.

I was so happy that tears started flowing immediately. I called the nurse, kissed him, and then I called Nique.

I guess that experience made him think about some things.

When they released him, I made sure that I was there to pick him up. When he got in the truck, he gave me directions on where to go. When we finally got to the address, it was a beautiful two-story, three-bedroom house.

"Welcome home, baby," Amir said.

I was silent for a while because I was trying to take it all in.

"Baby, what's wrong? You don't like it?"

"It's not that, baby. I love it. I just wasn't expecting it. When did you have time to do this?" I asked.

"I was going to surprise you for your birthday but shit happened. I'm new to this shit, Mina, so be patient wit a nigga," Amir said.

I just nodded my head as I took in what he was saying. I got out of the truck and went around to help him.

As we walked towards the front door, I was thinking, *what am I getting myself into?*

Phoenix

Chapter 9

I was the perfect woman. I took care of home while he was out taking care of business.

Before I knew it, three years had passed.

Things had changed drastically between me and Amir. I was still working at the shop, but only on the weekends. I was going to school full time to become a lawyer.

Amir was home less and when he was home, his phone was constantly ringing.

One night when Amir was home, I decided to give him a taste of his own medicine, so I called Nique.

"Hey, girl, I need a drink. Feel like going to Oasis?" I asked Nique when she answered the phone.

"I will be ready in an hour," Nique said.

"I will see you in an hour," I said, and then I ended the call.

I knew it wouldn't take me long to get ready, so I did some homework before I started getting ready.

After I showered, I put on a black oriental style mini dress with a pair of black stilettos with a chrome heel. I pulled my hair into a loose bun, leaving a few stray hairs out. I grabbed my clutch and was out.

I pulled up at Nique's. As soon as I walked in the door, Cas was on my ass.

"*Where* the fuck you going dressed like that?" Cas asked as soon as I walked in the house.

I rolled my eyes and said, "*Out.*"

"Did Amir see you? Naw, he couldn't have 'cause your ass wouldn't have made it out the house," he said as he shook his head from side to side.

"*Whatever,* Cason. Do you check him like this when he is out doin' him with these bitches out here?" I asked with my hands on my hips, waiting for an answer.

He didn't say anything. He just looked at me like I was crazy.

"*Exactly,* what I thought," I said as I walked away to go get Nique.

I didn't have to go far because she was just getting to the bottom step as I rounded the corner coming from the den.

"Look at you, hottie," I said as I stepped back to check her out.

She had on a black one piece with a deep V cut in the front. She was rocking a pair of gold stilettos and her hair was bone straight. By the time we reached the den so that she could kiss her man goodbye, he was gone.

She shrugged it off and we left the house.

***

We pulled up at Oasis at midnight. The line was practically down the block. We bypassed the line to go through the VIP door.

The club was jumping. We stopped at the bar first to get some shots. Then we found a table.

As soon as we sat down, a waiter came over to take our order.

"Hey, ladies, what are y'all drinking tonight?" she asked.

"Two shots of Patron and two apple martinis," Nique said.

"I will be right back with your drinks," she said, and then disappeared in a sea of people.

When our drinks came, we both took our shots and hit the dance floor. We were enjoying ourselves. We danced for three songs straight, and then went back to our table to catch our breath.

While we were sitting there, the waiter came over to our table with a bottle of Ace of Spades.

"Ladies, this from the gentleman in the corner," the waiter said as she placed the bottle and glasses down on the table.

Once she walked away, we looked over to the corner to see who the gentleman was. To my surprise, it was the guy Cas was talking to the day I got the truck.

We held up the glasses to say thank you.

Nique and I drank the entire bottle. We were feeling lovely by the time him and his friend came over to speak.

"Hey, Simeon. How are you? Thanks for the bottle," Nique slurred.

"Anything for you. Where's ya man at?" Simeon asked with a slight giggle.

"He better be at home waiting for me," Nique slurred as she pulled out her phone.

I giggled to myself as I watched her on the phone when Simeon approached me.

"Hello, my name is Simeon. How are you?" Simeon asked.

"I'm feeling lovely. Thank you for the bottle," I slightly slurred.

"I remember seeing you a while back. I didn't get the pleasure of getting your name that day," he said.

"*Damn,* you remember that? That was so long ago," I said with a slight giggle.

"Yea, ma, in my line of work you have to remember faces," he said.

"What kind of work do you do?" I asked.

"I'm a cleaner," he said.

"That doesn't sound too dangerous to me, but okay," I said as I took the last sip of my drink.

I discreetly gave Nique the signal that I was ready to go.

When I got up to leave, Simeon gently grabbed my arm.

"Ma, you just gon' leave like that and not give me your name?" Simeon asked.

"You will learn my name soon enough. Thanks again for the bottle," I said as I walked away.

We got in the car to leave, but I wasn't ready to go home.

I knew Nique was wondering what was going on, so I decided to surprise her with IHOP.

When we got there and were seated, she asked, "So what's going on, Bookworm? This isn't like you."

"Girl, Amir is getting on my nerves. I think he's cheating," I said just before the waiter arrived to take our order.

"With who? Why?" Nique asked once the waiter walked away.

"I have no idea with who or why. I am thinking about leaving him. I don't have time for the games he's playing," I somberly stated.

"Do what makes you happy. I peeped you and Simeon talking," she curiously stated.

"Girl, that wasn't about nothing. He was trying tho," I laughed a little as the waiter placed our food on the table.

"*Mmm hmm,*" Nique said as she cut her pancakes.

I didn't have much of an appetite. I played with my food as I watched Nique bash. When she was finished, I paid the bill and we left.

"You know I'm here if you need me," she said as I stopped in front of her house.

"I know. Thank you," I said as I turned to face her.

Damn, I want to kiss her. Now is not the time to be having

The Ultimate Betrayal

thoughts like this, I thought to myself as I looked at her lips. I bit my bottom lip as I watched her lips move, completely unaware of what she was saying.

I just want to reach over and kiss her lips. I want to work my way down and kiss each one of her succulent breasts, I thought as I felt my clit start to throb.

I snapped back to reality when I felt her hand touch my thigh. I looked up into her eyes and let the silence consume us.

"Mina, it will be alright," Nique said as she opened the door.

"Call me when you get home," she said, and then closed the door and went in the house.

I took the long way home just to kill more time. When I finally pulled up at the house, it was 5:30 am. I sent Nique a text.

Amina: *I made it home.*

Nique: *Okay ttyl*

I didn't bother to respond, so I put my phone back in my purse.

I slowly got out of the car and walked to the front door. I wasn't even in the house good before Amir started with the questions and accusations. I wasn't in the mood to argue. I walked straight upstairs to the bathroom and started the shower. Of course, he followed me.

While I was in the shower, he sat on the toilet smoking a blunt.

"Mina, where the *fuck* you been? I guess you're washing that nigga's scent off, huh?" he asked with a slight giggle.

"Just like your ass be washing them hoes' scents off of you," I exclaimed.

"So you were wit a nigga?" he aggressively asked.

"Don't worry about it," I said.

Thank god I was in the shower, I thought as tears started streaming from my eyes.

71

"*Fuck you mean* don't worry about it?" he gritted.

He snatched the shower door open and walked in.

"Like I said, don't worry about it. Shit, you out here fucking bitches while I'm at home waiting for you. Nigga, you ain't slick," I yelled.

"Mina, I'm not cheating on you. I'm out here getting this money so *we* can live, ma. I love *you*. I only want *you*," Amir said as he stepped closer to me.

"Yea fucking right, *Amir*. That's okay 'cause since *you* don't want me, I know a nigga that does. He's just waiting to take your place, so *I'm leaving*," I exclaimed.

Why did I say that? I thought as Amir backed me up against the shower wall.

"You gon' leave me, ma?" he asked.

I tried to push him out my way but he didn't budge.

"Yes, I'm leaving. *You* don't want me for real," I said looking him in the eyes.

"I do want you. I want you to be my wife. Fuck them bitches. It's about me and you," he said, stepping closer into my personal space.

"That's the problem. *You* fucking them bitches. So you don't need me. *Let me go*," I exclaimed as the tears were flowing freely down my face.

"So you gon' leave me?" he said as he kissed me on the neck.

"I love you, ma. Don't leave," he said as he kept getting lower with the kisses.

"Sex isn't going to fix this. Amir, I'm done. *I* don't deserve this," I moaned.

"You're the only woman for me," he said as he started playing with my pussy.

It felt so good but I was not about to give in. I tried to move his hand but he took my hands and held them above my head. He continued to play in my juice box.

"*Ohhhh, Amir,*" I moaned.

He released my hands and picked me up. He was eye level with my juice box. He didn't waste any time burying his face in my pussy.

I tried to squirm away but he sucked on my clit harder every time I moved.

"*Mmm. I love you. Don't leave me,*" he said between kisses to my clit.

"You don't love me," I moaned as I came in his mouth.

He unzipped his pants and pulled out his dick. Then he slid me all the way down on it. I couldn't help but moan. It felt so good.

"You gon' leave me, ma? I love you," he said as he stroked me slow and hard against the shower wall.

It hurt so damn good. My body started to shake as if I was having a seizure.

"*Oh my god. Amir. Amir. Amirrr,*" I screamed out as my love came down all over his dick.

Phoenix

Chapter 10

We stayed in the house all week reconnecting, completely ignoring the outside world.

It was six o'clock in the morning on Friday. Amir was knocked out from the way I put that thang on him. I couldn't sleep so I went to go sit on the deck in the backyard.

It feels good having Mir back, but how long will this last? Is this what he really wants? I wonder what he has planned for my 21st birthday, I thought as I watched the sun peek over the horizon.

"What's on your mind, baby?" Amir asked, bringing me out of my thoughts.

"Good morning. Nothing major, baby," I said as I looked up into his eyes.

"Come on, Bookworm, talk to me," he said as he slid behind me in the lawn chair. He wrapped his arms around me and kissed my forehead.

"What you getting me for my birthday, Mir?" I asked.

"Me," Amir said.

"Mir, stop playing," I said.

"I'm serious, baby girl. I'ma strip for you and all that," Amir laughed.

"Please don't," I laughed.

"What you saying?" he asked as he got up off the chair and stood in front of me.

"Nothing, baby," I said with a smirk, trying to pull him back down.

"So you don't wanna see me do this?" he asked as he began to grind.

Phoenix

"What about this?" he asked as he dropped his shorts and started swinging his tool and making it jump.

Cracking up laughing, I said, "Baby, stop. The neighbors might be watching."

"So, let 'em watch," he said as he approached me.

I was biting my bottom lip, anticipating his next move.

He dropped down to his knees and licked my kitty slowly.

"*Amir,*" I moaned lowly as I arched my back.

Suckling on my clit and gradually increasing the pressure had me trying to run.

"Mm hmm," he hummed on my clit.

"*Amir. Aaamirrr. I'm cumming,*" I moaned loudly as I squeezed his head between my thighs.

My body was shaking. He didn't give me any time to recover before he slid his swollen member deep inside me in one swift motion.

"*Oh god, Amir,*" I moaned as I held on to him tightly.

"Damn, you so wet," he moaned in my ear as he stroked me fast.

"Oh don't stop, daddy. Don't stop," I moaned and dug my nails into his back.

My juices were gushing out with each thrust.

"*Fuck, Amina,*" he moaned loudly as he went deeper.

I contracted my walls on his dick.

"*Mina. Mina. Mina,*" he growled as he coated my walls with his seed.

"Damn, baby. That is the best way to start the day," he said as he lay beside me.

"It is," I said snuggling up to him.

I wanted to stay like this but I knew we couldn't. We both had

76

to get back to our routines.

Things are going great but how long will it last? I asked myself.

After our little hiatus, we got back to our lives. Amir went back to work and I got back to my studies.

School was kicking my butt but quitting was not an option.

Amir was coming home every night, miraculously his phone didn't ring as much.

It seems that he can only be good three years at a time, I thought as I aimlessly looked around Casonique for an outfit to wear to my 21st birthday party tonight.

I should just go home and raid my closet. I know I have stuff in there I have yet to wear, I thought as I picked up a red corset and a pair of black leggings.

I went to the shop to get beautified.

"Hey, everybody," I said as I walked in.

I got a few waves and smiles as I walked to the shampoo area.

"Are you ready for tonight?" Nique asked as she draped the cape around me.

"Girl, yes, I need to unwind," I said as I laid back.

"I think my man got another three year itch. He's been back on the bullshit again," I said as she massaged my scalp.

"I don't know, Mina. You know how Mir is. But until you have proof, don't assume," Nique said as she washed and conditioned my hair.

"You have a point but I'm having a hard time trusting him," I said as I followed her back to her station.

"Don't let your paranoia ruin things. So what are we doing today?" she asked as she clipped my dead ends.

"I don't care. You can do whatever you want. Meet me at

Bistro when you close the shop," I said.

Maybe she's right. Maybe I am being paranoid. I'm not going to let this shit ruin my day, I told myself as Nique worked her magic on my head.

When I left the shop, it was eight o'clock. I had a few hours before my party so I called Farrah.

"Hey, boo. You want to grab a bite to eat before the party?" I asked when she answered.

"I was thinking we could all meet at your house and start the celebration," Farrah said.

"That's cool. Be there in an hour. I'm going to stop at the store," I said, then ended the call.

Before I put my phone away, I sent Nique a text letting her know about the new plan.

On my way home, I stopped at the store to grab some finger foods.

Once I left there, I went to the liquor store and got two pints of tequila. I was letting my hair down tonight.

When I got to the house, I was surprised to see that Amir was home. He'd been so busy lately. *Maybe I can get some before the girls get here,* I thought as I rushed in the house.

When I rushed through the front door, Amir was half sleep on the couch. I walked into the living room and immediately dropped down to my knees and took his limp dick into my mouth.

I felt it grow harder in my mouth as I went to work on his tool.

I sucked, slurped, hummed, and gagged on his member.

"*Shitttt,*" he moaned as he placed his hands on my head.

I was just getting good into it when the doorbell rang nonstop, followed by persistent knocks.

"Fuck that door, baby. Keep. Sucking. This. Dick. *Hmmm. Just.*

Like. That," he moaned.

I picked up the pace, tightening my jaws, making the head pop out of my mouth each time.

"Aaaah. Fuck. Let me. Fuck, baby. Let me hit that," he breathlessly moaned.

I shook my head no as I continued my assault on his tool.

"Fuck, Minaaa," he growled as he quenched my thirst.

"Mmm, that was good, daddy. Get the door for me. I'm about to shower," I said as I went upstairs to get in the shower.

"Really?" he said.

"Thank you, daddy," I tossed over my shoulder as I continued walking up the steps.

Amir

"What's up, Farrah. She just went to get in the shower. Make yourself at home," I said as I let her in.

"Hey, Amir. I must've interrupted something," Farrah said as she seductively eyed my semi erect member.

I followed Farrah's eyes and tried to hide my erection and get away from her. Before I could make my exit, she reached down and massaged my member.

"When you're ready for a *real* woman, you know where to find me," she said looking me in the eyes.

Damn, her hands are soft. This shit feels good. What the fuck is wrong wit me? Nigga, this ya girl cousin. Saved by the bell, I thought as it rang once and in walked Nique.

"What's up, Ni?" I said as I ran up the stairs to try and catch my baby in the shower.

"Baby, Ni and Farrah downstairs," I said as I walked into the bathroom.

"Mmmm shit," I faintly heard her moan.

"You need some help with that?" I asked as I got into the shower with her.

I pushed her up against the shower wall and entered her from behind. I didn't give a fuck about her hair getting messed up.

I stroked her fast and hard as the water beat down on our bodies.

"Amir .Amir. Shit. Right. There. Right. Fucking there," Mina screamed out as I beat it up.

"Right here? Right here?" I aggressively asked as I thrust in and out of her harder.

"Amir. Yes. Yes. Yasss. Shit, daddy, I'm cumming," Mina screamed out as her walls contracted and she came all over my dick.

I came shortly after her. We washed each other up, and then we got out of the shower.

Amina

"Baby, the limo will be here at 11:30. Be ready," Amir told me as he walked into my closet to get dressed.

"Okay, baby," I said as I threw some clothes on to go talk to my girls.

"Heyyy ladies," I greeted as I walked into the den.

"Don't hey us now. Where the drinks at?" Farrah stated with a smirk.

"Y'all ain't slick. We heard you slut," Nique said as she shoulder bumped me.

"That's why the bags are still in the car. I had to have my man and I couldn't wait," I said while laughing.

"It must've been good 'cause your hair is messed up. I would be mad 'cause I spent hours creating that style, but it's your birthday," Nique said.

"Ladies, we have to be ready in an hour. My baby said a car will be here at 11:30," I said.

"Well, let me go shower," Farrah said as she picked up her bags.

"Use the bathroom in the basement. Everything you need is down there," I said.

Since I'd had my shower already, I focused on my hair.

We finished getting ready just as the limo pulled up.

We all got into the limo. The champagne started flowing as soon as all our asses hit the seats.

"Baby, tonight is all about you. I love you. Happy birthday," Amir said as he clinked glasses with Farrah and Ni.

I had no idea what Mir had planned but I knew he went all out.

We pulled up at Oasis and I was surprised by what I saw. The red carpet was rolled out and photographers were everywhere. We sat in the limo people-watching for a minute before we got out.

Once we stepped out of the limo, cameras were flashing, I felt like a superstar.

Once we got inside the club, we went straight to the VIP section.

Patron, which happens to be my favorite drink, was on ice.

I was ready to party. Nique, Farrah, and I were taking shots. I was on a mission to get wasted.

We were dancing and laughing when I saw a familiar face with two other females approaching us. I didn't know where I knew her from, but I wasn't concerned with that. I gave my girls the heads up and we continued dancing.

We were ready for whatever if something popped off.

"Which one of you is Amina?"

"Why? Who wants to know?" Nique asked.

"*Bitch,* you know who I am. I am sure you know that *I've* been fucking Amir. I was here long before you. I just came to tell you that your time is up. We have a baby on the way. *We're* going to be a family," Keta said as she rubbed her stomach.

I laughed in her face and said, "Bitch *you're* old news. That baby probably isn't his just like the first one wasn't," I said as I stepped around Nique.

I guess she didn't like what I said. She tried to swing and missed.

I punched her in her face, busting her shit wide open.

"My nose. I'm going to kill you bitch," she said as she charged at me.

I hit her with a two piece and she went down like a sack of potatoes. Nique and Farrah looked at the other two bitches as they helped their friend up. I walked off to go find Amir because his ass had some explaining to do.

When I found him, he was surrounded by Cas and some other niggas but I didn't care.

"Who the fuck is this bitch talking 'bout she pregnant by you?" I yelled, looking him dead in the eyes.

He looked like a deer caught in headlights. He tried to play it cool.

"Baby, what are you talking about?" he said.

"Nigga, don't play wit me. I'll be right back cause the truth coming out tonight *trust,*" I said as I stormed off.

I walked straight to the bathroom to get the girl.

I snatched her ass up. She was begging me not to, but *fuck that.*

She should have thought about that before she opened her

fucking mouth.

When we reached Amir, I shoved her ass in the middle of his little crowd and said, "This is the bitch I'm talking about."

The look on his face said a million words.

"Mir, I'm sorry but this bitch need to know that you're leaving her so w-w-w-we can finally be a family," Keta stuttered.

"Keta, I told you I would deal with this after the blood test," Amir gritted.

"*Keta. Keta.* Are you fucking serious right now, Amir? Blood test? Nigga, is this *your* seed she carrying?" I asked.

"Amina, it's a possibility. I was going to tell you," Amir said.

"*When*? Nigga, you know what, that doesn't even matter. I can't believe this shit," I said as tears welled up in my eyes.

I refused to let my tears fall.

Farrah was trying to get me to leave but I wanted to hear the rest of this bullshit

"Mir, you know we been talking 'bout this for a long time. It's time we make it official. I am tired of your time being divided. Let her go. I am all you need," Keta cried.

"Keta there will never be an us again." Amir said.

"*Fuck you, Amir. I'm done,*" I said right before I walked away with Farrah and Nique fast on my heels. *Damn, what a way to celebrate,* I thought as I stood outside crying.

"Ma, you too sexy to be crying on your birthday," the familiar voice said.

I looked up into the eyes of Simeon.

"Happy birthday," he said as he handed me a box.

Just as I was about to open it, Nique and Farrah came out and led me away from the door.

I glanced back and mouthed thank you. All the while, I was

wondering how he knew it was my birthday.

Nique opened up the passenger door to my truck.

"Are you okay?" Farrah asked as she got in the backseat.

"I'm good, *fuck him,*" *I* said as I leaned back in the seat.

I closed my eyes, fighting back tears.

Nique kept quiet. She just turned up the music and drove.

Just before I closed my eyes, Nique hopped on the highway heading to Indianapolis.

I knew we would be on the road for at least two hours, so I went to sleep.

Chapter 11

When I woke up, we were in Indianapolis at Club Satisfaction. The line was long so we went VIP.

Once we got inside, I found us some seats at the bar and we started doing tequila shots. We were on our fourth shot when these fine ass dudes approached us.

"How you ladies doing tonight? My name is Maine and this my man, Hasaan," one of the dudes said.

He kissed each of our hands, letting his lips linger too long on my hand, so I snatched it back.

I rolled my eyes and said, "Fine."

I turned back around and Nique gave me a look that said, "Bitch, be nice."

"Excuse her, it's her birthday. She got some bad news today so she has a slight attitude," Farrah said.

I asked the bartender for another Apple Martini. As I got ready to pay for my drinks, Maine whispered, "Don't worry, ma, I got you. Don't punish me for what that nigga did. Happy birthday."

His voice was so sexy and his lips were so close to my earlobe, which happened to be my spot. If I would've had on panties they would've been flooded. I felt the moisture between my thighs. I knew I had to get away from this man before I threw it on him.

I got my composure and said, "Thank you."

I slid off the stool, grabbed Nique, who grabbed Farrah, and we hit the dance floor.

I was watching Maine's five foot eleven inch athletic frame with his smooth golden brown skin. He was fresh from his braids to his Jordan's, and he smelled good, too. He caught me staring at him and smiled at me. I smiled back.

I was eye fucking him as he watched me dance. Before we knew it, it was last call. Then the lights came on. I wasn't ready for the night to end, so we headed to IHOP.

After we were done eating, we decided to spend the night in Indy and do some shopping in the morning before we headed home.

When we got in the room, Nique called Cas to let him know we were safe and that she would be home tomorrow.

They stayed on the phone for an hour. I heard him say Amir was looking for me. After they said their I love yous, she ended the call.

Farrah disappeared. I wasn't worried because my cousin knew how to hold her own. I just wished she would've told us where she was going.

I was in my feelings blowing haze. *What did I do to make him cheat on me,* I thought out load.

I finally broke down and let the tears fall.

"You didn't do anything but love him," Nique said as she rubbed my back.

She let me cry on her shoulder. We blew haze until the sun came up. We ended up with a bad case of the munchies, so we decided to go to Walmart. On our way out, we ran into Maine and Hasaan.

I thought it was weird that they were there, but hey, to each its own.

They decided to tag along. We bought all kinds of snacks and we were out.

When we got back to the hotel, he slipped me a key and told me to come through if I couldn't sleep.

When we got back to our room, Nique and I drank everything in the mini bar.

I couldn't sleep. Farrah was still gone and Ni was knocked out.

I thought about what Maine said. I figured that since it was my birthday, I might as well enjoy it. So I showered and went to his room.

He was half asleep watching ESPN. I turned the television off and crawled on the bed. I started massaging his thick already hard penis. It had to be at least twelve inches.

He laid me down and started kissing my body as he undressed me.

When he got to my pussy, he planted sweet kisses all over it. Then he spread my lips apart. He kissed and nibbled on my clit as he fingered me. I was going bananas.

He had me climbing the wall just off his head game.

I miss Amir, I thought as I heard the condom wrapper open.

"Wait a minute. Maine, I can't do this," I said as I sat up.

"We're both grown. Ya man won't know," he said as he let out a frustrated sigh.

I instantly got nervous. *What was I thinking? This man could rape me. I should have took my ass to sleep,* I thought as I watched him move to the chair at the foot of the bed. *Lord, please watch over me,* I silently prayed.

"I'm not going to take it. It's cool. You know you're different," Maine said. "You got a nigga dick on brick. You sure you don't want me to put it in?" He slightly laughed, trying to hide his irritation as he slowly stroked his swollen member.

"I'm sure. I think," I said as I bit my bottom lip.

I loved to see a man pleasure himself.

He firmly stroked his tool while looking me in the eye. My clit was throbbing. I wanted feel him but I couldn't hurt Mir like that, so I just watched the show.

He moaned lowly as the pace of his stroke quickened, and then slowed back down.

"Touch it for me," he assertively whispered.

I lay back on the bed spread eagle. I took my right hand and placed it on my pussy. Slowly, I parted my lips and inserted one finger.

"*Ooohh Maine,*" I moaned as I looked into his eyes.

With my left hand, I tweaked my nipples from left to right.

Stroking faster, he moaned, "*Oh shit.*"

I was drunk with lust watching him stroke his massive tool as he walked towards me.

Fuck it, I gotta have this dick, I thought as I reached up and grabbed his tool.

I placed the mushroom shaped tip at my opening grinding on it. He put it in a little at a time until it was all in. Unable to speak, I gasped and dug my nails into his back. The harder he went, the deeper I dug.

"*Aaah, Maine. Fuck me,*" I moaned loudly.

He flipped me over and entered me from the back.

Pulling my hair, he began to moan. "*Throw. That. Ass. Back,*" he said with every thrust.

I threw my ass back on him fast and hard until he came and passed out.

This nigga can't be serious, I thought as I watched him snoring. I put on my stuff and went back to my room.

I tried to be quiet. When I opened the door, I went straight to the bathroom, showered, then climbed in the bed. I was about to close my eyes when two pillows landed on my head.

"Hoe, I hope you used protection," Nique and Farrah said in unison.

"I thought you were sleep. When did you get back?" I said through my laugh. Then I went to sleep.

When we finally got back to Tribeca, it was five o'clock Saturday evening.

I dropped Farrah and Nique off and headed home. When I got there, Amir's car wasn't there and his bags were by the door.

My first thought was *good he saved me the breath that I was going to use to tell him to leave.* But in reality, I wanted to beg him to stay.

Amir

"Man I fucked up big time!"

"I can't believe you started fucking Keta *again.* Nigga, what were you thinking?" Cas said as he lit a blunt.

"Nigga, it's so much shit goin' on. This is stress I don't need," I said as I took a double shot of Hen to the face.

"Nigga, I thought Mina was going to kill both of y'all. The look in her eyes was scary. I was nervous for you," Cas said laughing as he exhaled the Kush smoke and passed me the blunt.

"Man, that shit wasn't funny. I was nervous as fuck. Mina got a mean right hook tho. On some real shit, I gotta lay low for a while. Some shit just hasn't been feeling right lately," I said as I inhaled the smoke.

"The streets been talkin' 'bout some cat name Enzo. I got somebody workin' on that as we speak," Cas said.

"That's what's up. Man, some nigga tried to holla at me 'bout some work when I was in the mall. I looked at him like he was stupid, laughed at him, and walked away. These lil niggas need to learn the rules before they play the game, for real. I'm 'bout to head to the house so I can holla at Mina before I leave. I will call you when I get to where I'm going," I said as I gave Cas some dap.

Amina

With tears in my eyes, I walked back out the door and just sat in my car wondering what the fuck went wrong.

I got myself together and sped to Nique's house. When she opened the door, I broke down.

"Amir is leaving me," I said through the sobs.

"Have you talked to him?" Nique asked as she consoled me.

"No, I couldn't stay and watch him leave. I thought I was going to be the one to carry his baby," I sobbed.

"You need to talk to him," Nique said, hugging me.

I didn't want to be alone but I didn't want to be bothered, so I went to her guest room. I laid there silently crying until I fell asleep.

Amir

Damn, I fucked up, I thought as packed a few more items. I tried to call Amina but she wouldn't answer.

I didn't want to leave this way but I didn't have a choice. Before I could leave a message on her voicemail something hit me in the back of my head. I dropped the phone and shit went black, *damn.*

Amina

After hours of crying, I checked my phone and saw that I had a voicemail and a text message from Amir.

Damn, what have I done, I thought as I read the message he sent me. I continued to read the messages. I came across a message from Maine.

How the hell did he get my number, I asked myself as I got up to leave.

"Thanks guys. I'm 'bout to head home," I said to Nique and Cas as I headed out the door.

The normally ten minute drive home seemed long. I was surprised and happy to see Amir's car. I put on my game face but I was jumping for joy inside. My baby was home. He didn't leave.

We were going to work everything out.

When I opened the door, I noticed that the table in the foyer was flipped over. Some of his bags were gone and the hallway closet, which we called the vault and usually kept hidden, was ajar. Something didn't feel right in the house so I quietly backed out of the front door. I called Cas.

"Have you talked to Amir?" I asked, trying to sound as calm as possible.

"Not since earlier. Why?" he asked.

"His car was at the house but he wasn't. The vault was open and..." I said but was cut off immediately.

"Are you still at the house?" he asked.

"No. I am 'bout to pull in y'all driveway," I said as I turned into their driveway.

"You're staying here tonight," Cas said as he walked down the driveway to his car.

Amir

When I get out this shit, I'm goin' to kill this nigga and everybody involved. I hope them niggas didn't touch Mina. I can't believe they caught a nigga slipping, I thought as I looked around the room. I was torn away from my thoughts when the room door opened and in walked a familiar face.

What the fuck part of the game is this? I thought.

Amina

Five months had gone by and Amir was nowhere to be found.

I had run into Maine at the mall about two months ago and we'd been spending time with each other. He was the perfect gentleman, at least that was the vibe I was getting. I was starting to fall for him a little. I wasn't trying to be in a relationship with him. He was just cool to kick it with.

Nique and I were chilling at her house talking about Amir and, of course, girl stuff when the house phone rang.

The house phone was for business purposes only.

Nique slowly walked over to the phone, hesitantly pushed the speaker button, and said, "Hello."

"He's had enough time to get my money. Tell him the price went up. I want 3.5 mill in 24 hours or *else,"* the caller said. Then he hung up.

Immediately, Nique called Cas from the house phone.

"What's up, baby?" Cas said with concern.

"You need to come home *now,"* she said and hung up the phone.

We were startled when Cas appeared in the kitchen with us.

He crept through the garage door and Simeon came through the front, both with pistols in hand ready to shoot.

"Nique, how many boys came for the sleepover?" Cas asked speaking in code.

"None, baby," Nique said.

"We good. Simeon, check just to be sure. What's going on?"

Cas asked.

"You tell me, *Cason. Why do you need 3.5 mil by tomorrow?*" Nique asked.

"Fuck you mean 3.5? He said a mil and we were good?" Cas barked.

"Who is he? What's going on?" Nique asked.

"The nigga who snatched Mir. We have been searching high and low but the streets aren't talking," Cas said as he wiped his hand down his face.

"I'm starting to think my nigga dead," Cas added, putting his head down.

Hearing that, I began to feel faint. As if in a haze, I heard Cas say something before everything went black.

"Simeon, help me get her in the truck," Cas said with concern in his voice.

***

Beep. Beep. Beep. Beep.

Damn, what is that noise, I thought as I tried to open my eyes.

When I finally opened my eyes, I saw Nique asleep in a chair.

I tried to move but a sharp pain shot through me, which caused me to yelp. My yelp woke Nique.

Dominique

"Don't move, Bookworm," I said as I walked over to her bedside.

"What happen?" Mina asked as she tried to move again.

"Why didn't you tell us you were pregnant?" I asked.

"Pregnant. I didn't even know, Nique. Is my baby okay?" she

asked as tears filled her eyes.

"Girl, Lil Amir (AJ) is good. He looks just like Mir. Cas is in the nursery with him. He won't let nobody near him," I said with a slight giggle as I showed her pictures of the baby.

"Girl, you scared the hell out of us. You just passed out and we couldn't get you to wake up," I said as my eyes started watering.

"Why? How?" she asked as she reached and grabbed my hand.

"Dehydration. Fatigue. Stress. Mina, the baby was in distress so they had to do an emergency C- section," I said.

"How is he?" she asked.

"He's a fighter. He has underdeveloped lungs. They have him in an incubator in the NICU," I said as I gave her a hug.

Amina

After being in the hospital for a few days, I was finally able to see Lil Amir. The sight of him in that incubator made me cry. I wanted to hold him. All I could do was rub his tiny leg through the openings. After an hour of sitting in the NICU, I went back to my room and called Cas.

"How you feeling, ma?" Cas said.

"I am alive and so is my baby, so I can't complain," I said.

"You and Mir are strong so I know little man is a soldier," he said.

"Speaking of his father, we need to talk. What time you coming up here?" I asked.

"I will be there in an hour Mina," Cas said as he exhaled.

"A'ight," I said, and then hung up the phone.

Time was going by so slowly. The nurse gave me my meds and before I knew it, I was out.

When I woke up, Cas was there watching ESPN.

Ugh, I thought as I grabbed the call button and changed the channel.

"Come on, sis, turn back," he said.

I turned back so he could finish watching his show.

"Mina, I need to know exactly what you saw when you went home that night," Cas said.

"His car was there. The table in the foyer was turned over and the vault was partially open. Something didn't feel right so I called you and came back to y'all house"

"What didn't feel right, ma?" Cas asked.

"I don't know. I felt like I was being watched. What's going on?" I asked.

"Mina, you can't handle that right now. I promise I'll tell you when you come home," Cas said sincerely.

I was at a loss for words. I was blaming myself because if we were talking, he wouldn't have been there.

"Baby girl, don't worry, everything will be good," Cas hugged me and left.

I called Nique because I needed answers.

"Heyy, Bookworm. How you feeling?" Nique asked.

"I'm hanging in there. This pain ain't no punk," I said.

Nique laughed and said, "Quit being a baby. It couldn't hurt that bad."

"You'll see. I can't wait till your ass go through this. Give me the scoop 'cause I know you know what's going," I sassed playfully.

"When I leave the shop, I will be up there. What do you want to eat?" she asked.

"I'm not really hungry but you can bring me a cheese steak and a piece of strawberry cheesecake from The Factory," I said.

"Okay, see you in a lil bit," she said before she hung up.

Nique got there at about 8pm. I was starving and that hoe had the nerve to walk in empty-handed.

Dominique

"Hey, Bookworm. How's AJ?" I said when I walked in the room.

"Hey, Ni. He's making progress. I held him today. Where's my cheesecake tho?" Mina asked.

Laughing, I handed her the piece of cheesecake.

"Thank you," she said.

Taking a bite of the cheesecake, she said, "I will be released on Friday but AJ will have to stay until he can eat on his own."

"Are you coming to the house or going home?" I asked.

"I don't know, haven't decided yet. So spill it?" she said.

I walked out of the room and came back with a wheelchair. I grabbed her robe and we went downstairs. It was pretty outside and she really needed the fresh air.

"Well from what I heard, some nigga name Enzo got him. Nobody knows who he is or where he came from but he been murking niggas left and right, making his presence felt. He trying to run the city and then some."

"Why Mir tho? He been out the game for a minute, right?" she asked.

"Mina, I really don't know anymore," I said.

"He told me he was done. He said they were out. He said shit was getting deep and niggas was snitching left and right. He said they were getting out before somebody had kingpin ambitions and tried to bring them down," Mina said.

"I been trying to find out who Enzo is. None of the girls that come in the shop have ever heard of him. I don't know but you know I'mma find out. What's up with you and Maine?" I asked.

"Nothing really. I mean he's alright to chill with but I'm not trying to get into nothing serious because when Mir comes home it's a wrap," she said.

"Something is off with his boy, Hasaan. When I was talking to him, he was more interested in who my man was and what he did for a living," I said.

"That is weird. I am going to investigate that 'cause lord knows I don't need any more surprises," she said.

We shared a laugh as I agreed with her.

We talked some more, and then I took her back upstairs to her room.

Before I left, Mina told me that she was going to take a shower, get her medicine, check on AJ, and go to sleep.

Phoenix

Chapter 12

Amir

"Kela. What the fuck is this about?" I asked in shock as she placed a towel and a bag of clothes on the bed.

"You know what this is about. I'mma enjoy spending *your* money, nigga," she said as she leaned against the dresser.

"That's what this is about? Shit, you could have asked for some money," I said.

"Nigga, it's deeper than money," Kela said.

I couldn't do anything but laugh at her as I grabbed the towel and walked into the bathroom.

This cat is an amateur. He got his bitch watching me. This shit has got to be a joke, I thought as the water rained down on me.

I came up with a quick plan to get me out of there. I stayed in the shower until the water got cold.

When I came out of the bathroom, she was sitting on the bed talking on the phone. I took off the towel and started drying off, ignoring the fact that she was in the room. I took my time putting baby oil on. I knew she was looking because she could barely focus on her conversation.

I tossed her the baby oil gel so she could put it on my back. She ended her call and took her time oiling me up. I was thinking about the first time Mina and I made love. My dick was at attention and it was uncomfortable for me to continue laying on it, so I turned over.

"Ya man must not be packing like this," I said with a laugh.

"My man may not be as blessed as you, but he puts it down if you must know," she said as she looked at me lustfully.

"If he was putting it down, you wouldn't be drooling over mine," I said as I began to stroke my swollen member slowly.

"*Whatever,* you might have put it on Keta, but I'm not her," she said.

"Keta didn't tell you that she couldn't handle all this dick, huh?" I smirked as I bit my bottom lip.

"*I'm* not Keta. I can handle it," she said as took her skirt off.

That hoe didn't have on any panties. She tossed me a magnum. Thank god for that because there was no way in hell I was sticking my dick in her unprotected. Hell, I didn't want to do it at all. But, shit, I was not gon' let those mafuckas kill me.

They got me all the way fucked up. This nigga must not know who the fuck I am, I thought as I prepared to put it on her. I put my best moves on her. She was creaming all over my dick, calling me daddy and shit.

I was pounding her from the back while going through her purse. I found the .25 she had in a hidden compartment. I tucked it under the pillow and finished fucking her brains out. I got my nut after thirty minutes.

While she was in the bathroom washing up, I walked in and wrapped my arms around her waist. I kissed her neck, stepped back, and put a bullet in the back of her head.

I left Kela on the bathroom floor, wiped everything down, took her car, and dipped out.

I wanted to call Cas but I had to get to a safe place first. I went to the airport and bought a one way ticket to South Carolina.

When I touched down, I called Cas.

"My nigga better still be in one piece," Cas barked when he answered.

"I'm good. I don't know where a nigga at tho. I'm 'bout to find the nearest airport and head south. Meet me in South Caro *ASAP,"* I urgently stated.

I ended the call and swiftly made my way through the airport. Then I went to my house to wait on Cas.

Jermaine

I have been trying to be patient with Amina but I'm over all the bullshit. I should just kill her and try to find the money on my own. I mean I've already fucked so why won't she let me come through. I know that nigga stash is in the house, I thought as I waited on Hasaan to call.

All of these Tribeca niggas running around looking for Enzo, not knowing that I'm right in their faces. I need to get in touch with Mina so I can stay in the know of what's going on, I thought to myself as I answered the phone.

"What's the deal?" I asked.

"Kela is dead and Amir is *gone,"* Hasaan said.

"What the fuck you mean Kela is *dead?* That nigga Amir better be dead *too,"* I gritted into the phone.

"Enzo, he wasn't there when we got there," said Hasaan.

I exhaled slow and deep.

"Nigga, I swear if that nigga don't show up on the news *tonight,* y'all niggas gon' have to see *me.* That's my word," I said and hung up the phone.

Fuck. With Amir on the loose, I am a sitting duck. Amir is a killer and after what I tried to pull, I know he'll be coming for me. I just don't know when. I have to think of a new plan to get Amir's money, the connect, and more importantly, his life, I thought.

I needed to relax so I called Has back.

"Meet me at Clappers," I demanded. I ended the call before he could respond.

When I arrived at Clappers, Has was already there in VIP. I made my way to his section and ordered a couple bottles of Louis XIII. I got a few dances but I was waiting on Xstasy to come out.

I'd had my eye on her from day one, but she was so hung up on that nigga Amir that she didn't even notice me. Now my money was long enough to get her attention.

When she came out, she did her thing on the stage. I wanted to bend her over and fuck her right there, but I wasn't there for that at the moment. I was here to deliver the news about Kela.

I waited for Xstasy to finish her set then I met her at the bar.

"What's up, Keta, or should I call you Xstasy?" I said as I gave her a hug.

"Hey, Maine. You silly. I'm still Marketa," Keta said as she hugged me back.

"You look good. *Real* good. I need to holla at you about something," I said as we sat down at the bar.

"Let me get two shots of Hen. Keta, Kela was shot," I said right before the bartender set our drinks down.

"What you mean shot? Is she alright?" Keta asked as tears welled up in her eyes.

"She didn't make it," I solemnly stated.

"Maine, stop playing wit me. Where's Kela?" she said frantically.

I embraced her to calm her down as she cried.

"Keta, come on, let's get you out of here," I said as I escorted her out of the club to my car.

She gave me directions to her house. When we got there, I helped her out of the car and walked her to the door.

"Maine, can you stay with me tonight?" she asked.

"Yes," I said as we walked into her house.

We sat there drinking and reminiscing about the first time we met.

"Remember the night we met. You were trying to be cute on the block and busted your ass," I said smirking.

"Hell yea, my shit was sore for days. But you were the only one that didn't laugh. Amir and them were crying laughing," she said, shaking her head laughing.

"Yea, I came to help you up and you snapped on me like I was the one who made you fall," I said.

"Yea, I'm sorry about that. I was just embarrassed," she said.

We had a few more drinks. Then one thing led to another. The next thing I knew, Keta's mouth was wrapped around my dick.

She was giving me slow neck. Her mouth was cold and warm at the same time. I was loving the sensation.

She was massaging my balls and doing things with her tongue that sent chills through my body. I exploded in her mouth and she swallowed it all and started sucking my dick till it was hard again.

When I was at attention, I picked her up, slid my dick inside her walls, and carried her upstairs. She was bucking all over my dick as I carried her up the steps.

When we got to the top of the stairs, I put her up against the wall and stood up in the pussy. She was screaming my name, begging me not to stop.

I walked her to her room and when we landed on the bed, I put her legs on my shoulders and beat her guts up till she squirted all over me.

I got up and got in the shower. When I got out the shower, I told Keta what I had really been up to.

"Keta, it's my fault Kela is dead," I stated with a towel

wrapped around my waist.

"You killed her? Why?" she asked sadly looking at me.

"Have you heard of a nigga name Enzo? Well I'm him. Amir shot Kela and dipped," I said.

"Wait. Wait. Wait. *You're Enzo?*" she asked.

"Yes, I am, but you can't tell anybody. I'm about to take over these streets and I want you by my side," I exclaimed as I grabbed a blunt off of her nightstand.

I lit the blunt and said, "I know you want to see Amina fall from grace, so get down with me and let's take them both down."

I inhaled the exotic smoke while she let what I said sink in.

After Keta and I discussed the plan, fucked, and smoked a blunt, I took another shower and dipped out.

Chapter 13

Cason

"Baby, I have to fly south for a minute. I don't know when I'll be back. If you need me, you know how to reach me. I love you," I said on Nique's voicemail.

I boarded our jet and headed to South Carolina to check on Amir.

I didn't know what I was walking into so I was prepared and ready for whatever was about to jump off. My flight landed in SC at 10pm. Amir sent a car to come pick me up.

When I arrived at the house, I could tell he had been chain smoking blunts and shooting rounds. He only did that shit when he was beyond pissed and couldn't get his hands on the person that pissed him off.

I made sure I announced myself because that nigga had an itchy trigga finger.

"Damn, nigga, you snitching on me?" I said as I gave him a manly hug.

Laughing, he returned the gesture. He got serious when he said, "Death before dishonor. Guess who this nigga's bitch was?" he asked as he inhaled the Kush smoke.

"What you mean *was*? Who *was* she?" I asked.

"Nigga, I murked that bitch after I fucked," Amir said passing me the blunt.

"Damn, you fucked her then murked her? Her pussy must have been trash. Who *was* she tho?" I asked before I inhaled the exotic smoke.

"*Kela,*" Amir said.

"Keta loud mouth ass friend, Kela? Damn, she kept her mouth closed about that nigga. So who is this nigga? Do we know him?" I asked.

"Some weak ass nigga from the Nap. He's a brown skin nigga wit braids. He look familiar but I can't remember from where," he said.

"Will you know his face if you see him again?" I asked.

"Hell yea, I will know that nigga face. The next time I see him he's dead. I put that on my seed," he gritted.

"I need to tell you something. I know you're going to want to leave. Shit is too hot for you and I am sure she would rather have you alive than dead," I said.

I watched Amir's expression change from killer to worried.

"Amina was pregnant when you left. She gave birth to Lil Amir four months early. He is in the NICU and she will be released on Friday," I said.

"Damn, I'm a daddy. My baby gave me my first seed. Damn, shit is fucked up. I want to see her. I need to apologize and I need to see my lil man," Amir said as he smiled. "I'm a daddy. Nigga, I got a junior," he yelled excitedly.

"As soon as Mina and the baby are able to travel, I will fly them out here," I said.

"How is the baby?" he asked.

"His lungs aren't fully developed but he's good, fam," I said.

"Man, I gotta see my babies. Fam, I gotta see my little man and my lady," he said excitedly.

My nigga was happy. He was smiling and walking tall. He even teared up a little.

I will never forgive myself if something happens to him. But this is his first seed so we're going home, I thought to myself.

"Come on, fam," I said walking towards the door.

We got to the air strip just in time. The plane was still there. The pilot flew us back to the buckeye state.

We went straight to the hospital. I took Amir to the NICU. He sat with Lil Amir and had the nurse take some pics, swab his cheek, and do his foot prints.

After about an hour of being in there, I asked, "Are you ready to see Mina?"

"No, I can't face her right now," he said.

As we were getting on the elevator, Nique was getting off.

"Amir. Oh my god. Where have you been? Did you see the baby? Did you see Mina?" Nique asked excitedly.

She hugged him so tight. It felt good seeing my girl smile.

That smile soon turned into a frown. *"Don't you ever scare us like that again,"* she said as she punched him repeatedly.

"Baby, don't tell Mina yet. I will call you in a little bit. I love you," I said as I gave her a quick kiss.

Amir

Man, I couldn't bring myself to face Amina. I didn't know where to start. I didn't know what to say. To know that she was that close to me made me feel whole again. I didn't want to put her at risk any more than I already had.

I still can't believe that I am a father. I have to tie up all these loose ends 'cause I want to be there for my lil man, I thought.

"I couldn't do it, man. I couldn't face her. I can't lose her over some dumb shit. I gotta handle this first. Then I will fix shit with her. I couldn't live with myself if something happened to her, fam," I said sincerely.

"No need to explain, fam. I would have handled it the same

way if I was in your shoes 'cause niggas is grimey. Ain't no tellin' how connected that nigga is," Cas said.

***

When we got back to SC, we called the crew and had them meet us out there for an impromptu meeting. I needed them on their toes.

We talked about the Enzo nigga and all the shit that went down until everybody arrived. Yea, we were doing our thing but it wasn't an easy road to travel. We'd lost some good friends. Now we were making sure the ones that were still with us were taken care of to the fullest.

Man, I love the thrill of this shit, I feel like I am above the law, I thought.

We'd been doing it for so long, but I knew that one day the feds would try to get us. So we made enough money to buy up some businesses and houses. We went semi legit.

Amina had been begging me to get out the game but I wasn't ready until two years ago when I had to kill the nigga that put me and Cas on because he was snitching.

After that, I sat Cas down, we weighed our options, and the rest was history.

Two days later...
Dominique

"Hey, sexy mama, how you feeling?" I said as I walked into Mina's room.

"I'm good, wish my baby was going home with me," she said.

"Me too. He is so precious. He won't be in here for too much longer," I said.

I gave her a hug and started gathering her things and we left.

Before we went home, we stopped at Sake to get something to eat.

While we were watching the chef cook our food, I told her what had been going on.

"I wish Amir was here so he could see his son. I hope he's alive. Has Cas found out any new information?" she asked.

I didn't know what to say. I hated to lie to her.

"I don't know. He's been acting strange since Mir disappeared. He's in South Carolina now," I said.

"Nique, what if he's dead? He's been missing for five months," she asked sadly.

"Mina, I'm sure he's not dead. He could be just laying low till shit die down," I said.

"I don't know. This shit is crazy. I don't know what to do," Amina said.

"It's going to be okay. You'll get through this. *We'll* get through this together," I said.

The chef placed our food on the plate as the waiter brought our drinks.

We enjoyed our meal and finished our conversation. Then we left and hit a few stores.

When we got to the house, we watched movies until we feel asleep.

Phoenix

Chapter 14

Marketa

That bitch Amina took my security blanket from me.

If her young ass would have never been in the picture, I wouldn't be dancing for dollars. I would be living the good life with Amir by my side. I am going to make that hoe's life miserable, I thought as I left my twin sister, Kenyatta, a message.

"Ya-Ya, I need you to do me a favor. It's ten stacks in it for you. Call me back when you get this."

Damn, where is my sister when I need her, I thought as I hung up the phone.

I want in the kitchen in search of some snacks.

I was snacking on some grapes when Enzo called.

"Hello," I said.

"Are you working tonight? Are you good?" he asked.

"I'm alright," I said.

"Well I was just checking on you. I will call you later," he said.

I hung up the phone and the next thing I knew, he was at my door with Chinese food and Coronas.

We lay in bed, ate, and watched movies. For once, I felt wanted. It felt so good lying in his arms. I dozed off.

When I woke up, I got out of bed and headed toward the living room. I overheard Enzo on the phone.

"Baby, I miss you. You should let me come stay with you while you heal," he said.

"That's sweet but I'm good. Maybe we can meet for dinner or something," the woman said.

"Okay, baby, just let me know when and where," he said before he ended the call.

I hurried back to the bed and started flipping through the channels.

"Keta, I gotta go. I will holla at you later," he said. Then he kissed my forehead and bounced.

What the fuck is wrong with me? Whoever baby is she's about to lose her life. Fuck that, I'm not losing another baller, I thought as I held the pillow he'd laid on and inhaled his scent.

I grabbed my phone to call Ya-Ya again.

"What's good, twin?" I asked.

"Hello, Marketa. How may I help you?" she asked.

"I need you to do something for me," I said.

"Marketa, I don't have any money nor do I have a fiancé for you to borrow," Ya-Ya said angrily.

"*Seriously,* are you still mad about that? Ya-Ya, that was three years ago. It's not my fault he thought I was you. Let it go already," I said.

"Yes, I am still mad. You could've stopped him but the hoe in you just couldn't say no to the dick," Ya-Ya said.

"Look at it this way. If it wouldn't have been me, it would've been someone else," I stated matter-of-factly.

"*Whatever,* Keta, what do you want? You know that Amina had a baby and named him after Amir," she said.

"I know, that's why I'm calling. I need you to make Lil Amir a memory," I said.

"What's in it for me?" Ya-Ya asked.

"Ten stacks," I said.

"I want my money, too," said Ya-Ya.

"Come to the club tonight. Bring proof," I said.

"You'll have your proof. Make sure you have my money.

Later," Ya-Ya said.

I hung up the phone smiling as I laid back, still holding Maine's pillow.

Kenyatta

Little did my sister know, I was about to pay her back for the pain and humiliation she'd caused me.

Little Amir was my meal ticket to the good life. I would never have to work again. I sent the nurse who was assigned to him on a dummy mission so I could switch the babies and make my escape.

It must've been fate because I had helped deliver a stillborn that morning. I grabbed Baby Doe and placed him in the incubator Amir Jr. was in.

Simeon is going to be so proud of me, I thought as I made the switch.

The code was being called as I closed my office door. The usual five steps from my door to the elevator felt like I was walking a country mile.

As I waited for the elevator, it felt as though all eyes were on me.

I heard someone calling my name in the distance. When I turned to see who it was, my heart dropped. The doors opened and I rushed onto the elevator.

I breathed a sigh of relief as I watched the head of security and the charge nurse disappear on the other side of the doors. Once I reached the garage, I put my things in the car and sped to the airport. I called Keta from the airport.

"Wire the money to my account. I will text you proof that's it done," I said. I ended the call and sent a pic of Baby Doe.

Once that was done I grabbed my bags and walked into the

113

airport.

I walked up to the ticket counter and said, "I need a one way ticket to Cancun, Mexico, please."

"Ma'am, is it just you?" the cashier asked.

"I have an infant. Will there be a charge for him?" I asked as I showed her the baby.

"No, ma'am. He is so adorable. Would you like to travel in first class?" he asked.

"Yes, I would. Thank you," I said. I handed the older gentleman my credit card and driver's license.

Thank god I am a twin, I thought as he looked over my information and entered it into the computer.

I was nervous as hell.

I can't believe Keta wanted me to kill this precious baby. All of this over some dick. I refuse to let an innocent baby get harmed over her bitterness. I wonder how she's going to feel when she finds out I tricked her, I thought as I waited to board my flight.

Dominique

"Mina, get up. We gotta go," I said as tears streamed down my face.

"Nique, what's wrong? Who was that on the phone?" Mina asked.

I ignored her questions and headed towards the door. I said, "We have to go, *now.*"

Once she was in the car, I explained the situation to her. She had more questions, but I had no answers. When we got to the hospital, we went straight to the NICU, where we were escorted to a private room.

We waited for about five minutes.

The doctor came in and said, "Ms. Reynolds, I'm sorry but Amir Jr. died from an intraventricular hemorrhage. You have my deepest sympathies."

He walked out of the room, leaving us with questions.

"Oh my god. Why?" Mina screamed as she fell to her knees on the floor.

I got down there and held her as we cried together.

"Nique, I need to see my baby. He can't be gone," Mina said.

Amina

I broke down. My little man was gone. I couldn't believe it.

I asked the nurse if I could see him one last time. She took us back to the room where they had him. When she removed the sheet, I looked at the lifeless infant and tears instantly started flowing.

"Oh my god," I said.

I collapsed in Nique's arms.

"Ma'am, I am sorry for your loss. We tried everything to save him but our attempts failed," the nurse said.

"Nique, that's not my baby," I said.

Nique just ignored me. We stayed with him until the funeral home came and got him.

Dominique

"Cas, I need you and Amir to come home. AJ died," I said through sobs.

"Nique, what happen?" he asked.

"Cas, I don't know. He was doing fine when we left. We got a call this afternoon saying he was gone. Cas, the shit just don't feel right," I said.

"Calm down, ma, you gotta be strong for Mina right now.

Where is she at?"

"Sh-she's in Amir's nursery. She won't come out of there. She keeps saying that's not her baby," I cried.

"I'm on the next flight there. I love you," Cas said.

I hung up the phone. I walked upstairs and tried to talk to Mina but she didn't respond. I decided to give her some time alone so I went past the shop to collect booth rent and make sure shit was running smoothly.

I was going to be off for a while, so I left Kema in charge.

I went past the funeral home to finish making the arrangements for AJ's funeral. When I was about to head to the house, Cas called, so I went to get him from the airport.

Amina

Damn, who the fuck is knocking on the door like the fucking police, I thought as I raced down the stairs to give whoever it was a piece of my mind

"Why the fuck are you beating on my fucking do..."

I stopped midsentence because I was surprised to see Maine standing on my doorstep with flowers.

Ugh more flowers, how the fuck did this nigga find out where I live because I never told him, I thought as I looked at him like he had two heads.

"What are you doin' here? How you know where I live?" I asked with an attitude.

"Bae, I didn't think you would be mad. I ran into Nique. She told me. *Damn,* you not happy to see a nigga?" Maine asked with a nervous giggle.

"It's not that I'm not happy to see you. I'm just not in the mood for company. I lost my son today," I solemnly stated.

"That's cool, ma. These flowers are for you. I just wanted to see you and hear your voice. You don't have to go through this alone. Let ya man in," Maine said.

I took the flowers from him. I was starting to feel bad but something didn't feel right so I promised him that we would spend some time together tomorrow and he left. Once I closed the door and locked it, I checked all the other doors and windows in the house and called Nique.

"Did you see Maine today?" I asked.

"No, why?" she asked.

"This nigga just showed up at my door. Bitch, something didn't feel right when he was here so I sent him on his way," I exclaimed.

"You know I don't fuck wit him like that. Are you straight tho?" she asked.

"I'm good. I was just checking. I will call if I need you," I said, and then ended the call.

Meanwhile, unbeknownst to me, Simeon and Maine were having a meeting of the minds.

This shit is getting crazy. I don't know if Amir is dead or alive and I burying somebody's baby in two days. I know that ain't Lil Amir, I thought.

I called Maine to get to the bottom of how he found out where I lived. He told me he followed me one day. *Damn, I was slipping,* I thought as I hung up the phone.

Phoenix

Chapter 15

Simeon

How the fuck this nigga find out where she live, I thought as I listened to Ya-Ya. I watched the exchange between Amina and Maine. The look on her face told me that she wasn't too happy to see him.

I ended my call with Ya-Ya, pulled my Nina out, and snatched Maine's ass up.

"Nigga, what the fuck you doing here?" I barked as I put my pistol to his head.

"I came to check on my girl. Who the fuck are you?" he asked nervously.

"I'm her guardian angel that's all you need to know. Don't let me catch your ass around here again 'cause the next time I see you, I won't be so nice," I said.

I let him go and walked back to my car.

I didn't even bother keeping my eye on him because I knew that nigga was shook. Once I was inside my car, I made sure he left.

This was my chance. I hopped out of the car and made my presence known.

Knock. Knock. Knock.

Amina

Ugh, I just told him I didn't want to be bothered, I thought as I snatched the door open. I was about to ask him if he was hard of hearing, but I didn't get a chance to because the man before me wasn't Maine. It was Simeon's sexy ass.

I didn't know what to say. I was embarrassed. I looked a mess. I wanted to slam the door and hide, but I was stuck.

He was looking so good. He was rocking some dark denim jeans, a white polo shirt, some fresh white uptowns, and his dreads were down under his navy blue 59/50 Yankee hat.

"What's up, ma? How you feeling?" he asked.

Hearing his voice brought me out of my daydream.

"Hi, Simeon, sorry 'bout that. I thought you were somebody else. Come in," I said.

I moved to the side to let him in. as he walked by me, his cologne invaded my nostrils and caused a flood in my panties.

Simeon was five-foot eleven. He was slim, but not too skinny. He had a burnt sienna complexion and his dreads were black with reddish blonde tips.

He had piercing green eyes. I locked the door and headed towards the kitchen.

"Do you want anything to drink?" I asked as I walked past the living room.

"No, ma, I'm good," he said.

I was at ease since Simeon was there. I figured Cas must've sent him. I didn't know what Maine was up to.

I grabbed a bottled water out the fridge and headed towards the living room. I stood in the entryway for a moment and watched Simeon flip through the channels.

"So what brings you to my neck of the woods?" I asked as I plopped down on the couch.

"Cas sent me over here to check on you," he said.

"Damn, I thought maybe you just wanted to see me," I said as I giggled.

"Amina, you silly. You be playin' a nigga. I figured since you fuck wit that bum ass nigga you wasn't checking for me," he said. *Damn, don't nobody like this nigga. I wonder why,* I thought as I took a sip of my water. I decided to pick his brain to see what he was about because he may have dressed hood, but something told me that he wasn't hood.

"So, Simeon, what's your story?" I asked as I turned to face him.

I am from Newark, NJ. I grew up in the suburbs. My mom is a doctor and my father was lawyer. I came to the Midwest to attend school and expand my business. I am your typical stereotype of a spoiled little rich kid in love with the fast life. Can I get that drink now?" Simeon said with a nervous giggle.

"Sure, what would you like? Sounds like there's more to the story but you don't have to tell me tonight," I said.

I got up off the couch and made him a rum and coke.

We continued talking and, before we knew it, it was ten o'clock pm and we were both hungry. I didn't feel like going out and neither did he, so we ordered some pizza and wings.

We played some video games, talked, and watched movies. We were watching *Paid in Full* and I snuggled up next to him and fell asleep.

Simeon
I wasn't expecting this to turn into an all-day thing. Shorty is cool as hell.

I didn't want to leave, but I can't let that keep me from carrying out my plan. It took me years to get in this position. I wished I would've been able to tell Amina the *whole* truth about my life.

I watched her as she slept. She was so beautiful.

It was around 2am when I felt her stirring. I pretended to be sleep when she got up off the couch. She stretched and then I felt the light taps on my arm. I stirred a lil but I didn't open my eyes immediately. After a few more light taps, I decided to open my eyes.

"What's up, ma, you good?" I asked.

"Yea, I was starting to get uncomfortable. I am about to get in the bed. You're more than welcome to sleep in the guest room," she said.

I accepted the offer because a nigga was tired.

She led me to the room next to hers. I kissed her on the cheek and we parted ways.

I was laying there flipping through the channels when I heard Amina moving around her room singing. I began to imagine her riding my dick, her ass slowly bouncing up and down.

Damn, I thought as I shook my head and adjusted my dick.

I laid there listening to her sing and move around her room. I was drifting off to sleep when I heard soft moans. I thought I was tripping till they got a little louder.

I crept out of bed and slowly walked out the door into the hallway. Her door was slightly ajar. I could see her lying on the bed spread eagle playing with her bubblegum pink pussy.

My dick was at full attention as I watched her tweak her right nipple, then her left, while she used her left hand to rub on her clit and fuck herself.

She was grinding on her fingers as her moans were getting louder and louder. By the way she was grinding, I could tell she was on the verge of cumming.

It took everything in me not to go in there and tear that pussy up. I stayed in the shadows and watched her body spasm as she grabbed the sheets with her right hand. She called out my name as she climaxed.

After that show, I waited a few moments before I went into the bathroom and took a long shower.

I have to have her, but will she have me? Only time will tell, I thought as I let the water relax my body and ease my mind.

Amina

Damn, I hope he didn't hear me. I can't believe I said his name, I thought as I got up to go clean myself up.

When I was done, I crawled in the bed and attempted to go to sleep.

I heard Simeon go to the bathroom. Then I heard the shower start. I fought the urge to join him. I turned on a movie and fell asleep.

I woke up at 7am because I had a few errands to run before I met Maine. I decided to cook breakfast for Simeon. I made French toast, cheese eggs, bacon, grits, and some orange juice.

Damn, I hadn't cooked like that since Amir. My mind drifted off to happier times as I fixed his plate, and then mine. I was so deep in my thoughts that I didn't even notice Simeon standing in the doorway watching me.

"Good morning, beautiful," he said.

His voice startled me and I almost spilled the juice.

"Good morning, how did you sleep?" I asked.

"I haven't slept that good in a while. I didn't want to get up but my stomach growled so loud that it woke me up, so I followed my nose," he said.

"You so silly. There's your plate. Sit down and eat before it gets cold. What you got planned for today?" I asked.

Before he could answer, my phone rang. It was Nique so I answered.

"Good morning, sunshine," I spoke cheerfully.

"Mmmm, good morning. What the hell you so chipper about? What you doing? What time will you be here?" she rambled.

"Damn, detective, if you must know, I am eating breakfast with a friend. I feel bad about how I did Maine so I'm going to do lunch with him. I will be there at 1:30. Your ass better be ready too," I said while laughing. I knew she was about to ask twenty-one questions but I stopped her.

"Well I am being rude so I will see you later. Love you, later," I laughed.

"Amina don't you..." was all I heard because I ended the call and finished enjoying Simeon while I had him for the moment.

The more I learned about Simeon, the more I wanted him.

He told me that he wanted a family one day and he had plans of opening his own business, as well as getting some real estate.

The time went by fast. After I got ready, he promised to call me later. As we walked out the door, he walked me to my truck, kissed me on the cheek, and waited for me to pull off.

As I pulled off, I called Maine to confirm our lunch date and let him know I was on my way.

***

The whole time I was with Maine, I felt like somebody was watching us. But when I looked around, nobody seemed out of place. I guess I was just being paranoid.

I ended the outing early because I wasn't feeling it. Then I called Nique.

"Hey, girl, I know it's early but I'm headed your way," I said.

"That's cool. How did lunch go?" she asked.

"I will tell you about it when I get there. I will see you in forty five minutes," I said.

I ended the call. The whole ride to Nique's, I was deep in thought about the things going on in my life that I didn't notice the smoke gray Crown Vic with limo tint following me.

Amir

Damn, did she set me up? Is that my baby she about to bury? What the fuck is going on? I thought as I watched Amina and Enzo on a date.

I wanted to grab both their asses and take them to the panic room. Somemafuckingbody got some explaining to do. I continued smoking my blunt, trying to calm my nerves, but the sight of him touching my wife was burning me up.

I decided to leave and head to the Nap to get some more info on this Enzo nigga.

"Dog, I'm on my way. You got that for me?" I asked.

"Yea, nigga, I told you I got you," Keys said.

I ended the call and turned the radio up. I made the two hour ride in half the time.

When I got to Keys, he ran down who Enzo, aka Maine, was and then it dawned on me who he was.

I laughed to myself because that nigga should have killed me when he took me from my house.

I'm 'bout to torture him and everybody that is associated with this takeover attempt, I told myself.

When I jumped on the highway headed back Tribeca, I called Cas.

"Yo I'm heading back south to lay low for a minute. I will stay in touch," I said.

I ended the call thinking of a plan to expose all the snakes in my grass.

When I got back to Tribeca, I went to view Lil Amir's body. I didn't feel like I was losing a son. That little boy wasn't mine and I had the DNA to prove it.

"I'm going to kill that bitch," I said as I read the DNA results again.

Simeon

"How was your flight?" I asked.

"It was fine. The precious cargo is sleeping now," Ya-Ya said.

"That's good to know. I will send the rest of that money in the morning," I said.

"No need to rush. Baby, I trust you," she said.

"I know, ma, I just don't want you and lil man to go without," I said.

"I love that in you. When are you joining us?" Ya-Ya asked.

"I don't know. Shit bout to be ugly. I'mma make something happen soon. I gotta go, talk to you soon," I said.

I hung up the phone and lit another Kush blunt.

These niggas so worried about Enzo when they should be worried 'bout me, I thought as I blew smoke out of my nose.

Fuck these pussies, mi gun blaze fire pon dem wen dem least expect it. Wen di smoke clear I will be di *onli* king still standing.

Chapter 16

Dominique

I can't believe that slut hung up on me. I wonder who her friend is. I wonder if she got rid of Maine's tired ass, I thought to myself as I put the finishing touches on my hair and make-up.

With all the stuff that she is going through right now, she needs a distraction. I can't believe we are burying Lil Amir tomorrow.

I was holding back tears when I looked up and saw Cas watching me. I guess he read my mind. He came over and held me. Cas was my heart, he was my backbone when I was not strong. I loved that man with all my heart.

"I love you, ma," he said, bringing me out of my daydream.

"I love you, too," I said.

We kissed, then his phone rang and he disappeared.

I tried to ear hustle but I saw Mina pulling up as I descended the steps, so I headed straight out door. Once I got in the truck, I started firing off questions. But first I had to read miss girl for hanging up on me.

"Heifer, if you ever hang up on me again, I will be at your door before you can get the phone closed all the way to kick ya ass. This nigga must be something special. He got you hanging up on me," I said as I climbed in the truck.

"So who is he? What does he do? Where did y'all meet? How long y'all been talking?" I asked.

"Slow down, damn. He ain't nobody special. I've been seeing him around a lot but more lately, since all this shit been going on," she said.

She kept her eyes on the road but I knew she felt me burning a hole in the side of her head.

"It was Simeon," she blushed.

"*What?* Yea right. Girl, he is fine. He must have put it on you. He had your ass up cooking breakfast," I said with a giggle.

"We didn't have sex. I'm trying to figure out the situation with Maine. We were just kicking shit then we fell asleep. I am starting to feel Simeon, but we can only be friends and I am cool with that," she said.

I rolled my eyes. I couldn't stand Maine's ass, especially after that shit he pulled yesterday.

We chopped it up some more. I gave her the run down on what had been going at the shop and I told her that everybody sent their sympathy. She told me to tell them thank you. Then we rode in silence, each of us in our own thoughts.

I could see the pain all over Amina's face. I didn't know what she was going through but I could see that it is starting to take its toll on her.

When this all over, I am going to talk Cas into sending us to Jamaica for a week or two. A smile spread across my face at the thought of getting away for a while.

When we pulled up at the mall, we got out of the truck. I walked over and gave Amina a hug.

"I love you and I am here whenever you need me. You not going through this alone," I said.

"Thank you. I love you, too. People gon' think we gay if you don't let go," she said with a laugh.

I let her go and we walked inside the mall. *Just gotta love that girl,* I thought.

We tore the mall down. We had so many bags that we paid

128

some young boys to help us carry them to the truck. *Ain't nothing like some retail therapy to temporarily ease your mind,* I mused as we headed for the truck.

Once all the bags were inside the truck, we went back in to grab something to eat. Then we went and got our nails and feet done. We could've gone to the shop, but I knew they were going to be asking a thousand questions. I knew one of them bitches would have said the wrong thing and it would've been all that she wrote.

While we were in the salon, Keta stank ass walked in. *Ugh, just when I thought this was going to be a drama free day,* I thought as I watched her walking our way.

"Sorry for your loss," Keta said.

Amina just gave her a look. So I said," Thank you," as she turned to walk away.

I was surprised that she did that and something about her new appearance made me suspicious. Don't get me wrong, Keta kept herself together. She was always fresh, rocking the exclusive hood shit, but today she looked like the spokeswoman for Gucci.

I made a mental note about that.

"Why you igg her like that?" I asked.

"Fuck that snake ass bitch. She didn't mean that shit. She was being funny," Mina said.

"Maybe she did, but fuck her if she didn't. What you getting into tonight?" I asked.

"Probably nothing. Maine wants to see me. But after that shit yesterday, I don't know. I might hit Simeon up," she said slyly.

"Yea, I feel you on that. Something is up wit him. I just don't know what. Look at you," I said as the lady finished working on my feet.

After that was done, she dropped me off at home.

I knew it was going to be a long day tomorrow.

Jermaine

I been calling Amina all day and she been ignoring me. Damn, I think I played my hand too soon by showing up at her house, I thought as I rolled a blunt and kicked shit with my nigga Hasaan.

"Nigga, what we gon' do? You out here falling in love and shit. Did you forget what we came to do?" Has asked.

"Naw, Has, I haven't forgot. I am working on that. Nigga, I ain't in love. It took everything in me not to knock that bitch out and force her to show me the safe and give up the connect when I went over there," I said as lit the blunt.

"Man, I told you not to expose yourself yet. Why the fuck she never told you where she lay her head anyway?" Has asked as he inhaled the weed smoke.

"Fuck if I know, but I'mma get in there. We gon get this money by any means necessary. You know how I get down. Tomorrow is going to be the day I get in, trust me."

"Yea a'ight, nigga, we'll see. Isn't tomorrow that lil nigga funeral?" Has said as he took a pull on the blunt.

Before I could respond, my phone started ringing. I thought it was Amina but it was Keta's thirsty ass. She was a'ight but she seemed to be too damn needy.

I exhaled hard before I answered, "Hello."

"Hey, baby, I miss you," Keta purred.

"What's up wit you?" I asked.

"I'm at the mall doing a little shopping. What we doing tonight?" she asked.

"You should be working tonight, right? Me and Has might slide through the club later. I'm about finish handling this business. I will get up with you," I said.

I hung up the phone, took the blunt from Has, and got lost in my thoughts.

"A'ight, man, this the game plan. I'mma add another element to this team, Keta. She used to fuck wit Amir hard and I know she know some shit Amina not telling me. So I'mma see what I can get out of her. I want you and Kareem to keep them bitches in y'all eyesight when I'm not around," I ordered.

"I feel what you saying, but them hoes don't do nothing but shop. Ya girl be spending light if she holding all that paper. I think Cas is the one wit all the money. I say we kidnap both them bitches and see how much they're worth," Has said.

"Nigga, that's plan B if this shit don't pan out 'cause my patience is wearing thin," I said as I put the roach out.

Around 11pm, Keta called me.

"Hey, baby, me and few girls from the club are 'bout to chill at my place. You and your boys should come thru," she said.

"We might come thru there. Why aren't you at work?" I asked like I really gave a fuck.

"I wanted to chill with you so I took the night off, baby," she cooed.

"Don't miss no money for me, you should've took your ass to work. I will see you later," I said, and then ended the call.

Me, Has, and a few other niggas we fuck wit went over to Keta's. Drinks were flowing, blunts were in rotation, and asses were clapping. We were chilling, having a good time. Keta was giving me a lap dance when Amina called.

"What's up?" I greeted.

"Nothing much, missing you," Amina said.

"*Word?*" I said shocked.

"Yea, I owe you an apology," Amina said.

"Big daddy, get off the phone. Momma wants to play," Keta said as she slid down to eye level with my dick.

I was hoping Amina didn't hear it but the silence on the other end of the phone told me she did.

"*Fuck.*" I said as I pushed Keta off of me and walked outside.

I tried to call Amina back but she wouldn't answer the phone.

Keta came outside to find me. When she found me, she started playing with my zipper. When she found what she was looking for, she wrapped her warm mouth around my tool and she sucked it like her life depended on it.

I dropped my phone and forgot all about my future woman, Amina.

Chapter 17

Amina

I finally decided to call Maine and that nigga was with some bitch. Instead of arguing with him, I hung up. Of course he called right back but I wasn't in the mood for the shit.

I decided to call Simeon because I didn't feel like being alone.

"Hey, Simeon. Are you busy?" I asked.

"I'm never too busy for you. What's up?" Simeon said.

"I don't want to be alone. I was wondering if you felt like hanging out," I asked.

"Give me a half hour," he said.

"See you then," I said, and then ended the call.

Since I had some time before he got there, I decided to cook. I made smothered chicken, rice, greens, cornbread, and red velvet cake for dessert.

I didn't have enough time to shower before he got there, so I had to wait.

Lord knows what would happen if I opened the door wrapped in a towel, I thought as I heard Simeon knocking at the door.

"Hi. Thank you for coming," I said as I stepped aside to let him in.

I gave him a hug after I hung his jacket up on the hook.

"Thank you for having me," he said as he hugged me back.

I led him to the kitchen, where I prepared our plates.

"Where's your boy Maine at?" he asked as he took a bite of chicken.

"I don't want to talk or think about him right now. I have to bury a baby, my baby, tomorrow. Mir's missing. Why is this happening to me?" I asked.

Simeon saw the pain in my eyes. He reached out for me and I collapsed in his arms and broke down. Simeon held me until the tears stopped. He carried me to the bathroom, cleaned me up, and then carried me to my bed.

He cuddled next to me till I fell asleep. When I woke up, it was 3am. I was headed to the bathroom when I heard a noise behind me. I grabbed my .25 out the vase in the hall.

"Make one wrong move and I'm sending you home," I gritted.

"Amina, it's me. Ma, put the heat down. I was coming to check on you," he said calmly.

"Simeon, *damn,* I forgot you were here. I'm sorry," I said.

I placed the gun back in its hiding place. Then I walked in the bathroom.

When I opened the door, Simeon was standing there cracking up.

"What's so funny?" I asked.

"Shit, you don't need a gun if you wake up looking like that. All you have to do is turn on the light and I'm sure a mufucka would run the other way," he laughed.

I went back in the bathroom and looked in the mirror. My hair was standing straight up. I looked a hot mess. I was a little embarrassed.

I focused on Simeon towering over me in the mirror and we looked good together. *I wonder what his sex game is like.* I quickly got the thought out of my head.

"Shut up, Simeon," I said as I punched him in the arm.

"Okay, wild woman, you got it," he said throwing his hands up.

I pushed him out of the bathroom so I could wrap my hair.

When I came out, Simeon was sound asleep in my bed. *This*

nigga think he slick, I thought as I climbed in the bed.

I snuggled up close to him and went back to sleep. It felt good to be held. I just wished it was *my* man holding me. It seemed like no sooner than I closed my eyes, the alarm clock went off and the phone started ringing.

I turned the alarm off as I answered the phone.

"Hello," I said groggily.

"How you feeling this morning?" Nique asked.

"I'm just here, Nique. I don't feel like that's my baby. God wouldn't punish me like that," I said wearily.

"I know it's going to be hard but you gotta do it. I will be there for you every step of the way. We are on our way to your house. We'll let ourselves in. The limo will be there at 10am. Lay back down. I will wake you when I get there. Love you, see you in little bit," Nique said.

"Love you too, and thank you so much," I said.

I hung up the phone and snuggled back up in Simeon's arms.

The Funeral

"Amir Carter Jr. was an angel, my angel. Although he wasn't on this earth long, I knew that he was destined..." Amina's words caught in her throat as she locked eyes with Amir.

All eyes were on him as he slowly made his way down the aisle.

There were a few gasps and whispers as he walked past the casket without looking into it.

His mind state was *fuck it, it's not my loss to mourn.* Every step he took pissed him off even more. When he finally reached the podium, Amina tried to wrap her arms around him but he stopped her.

"Bitch, whose baby is that?" he gritted.

The confused look on Amina's face should have told him that she didn't know what he was talking about.

To him, that could've all been an act.

She was shocked he would come at her like that. She was about to respond but the next thing she knew, she was against the wall with his hands around her neck.

"Who baby is that, Amina?" Amir yelled at her as he tightened his grip.

She was struggling to get away. It was becoming harder for her to breath. She gave up the struggle and just looked into Amir's eyes as he choked the life out of her.

As a shot went off, Cas and Simeon finally got him off of Amina and she fell to the ground gasping for air.

Dominique

What the hell is going on, I thought as I watched my cousin choke the life out of my best friend. *Lord forgive me for what I'm about to do,* I silently prayed.

I raised my .25 in the air and fired a shot. That cleared the church and got Amir to drop Mina.

Amina

Thank God for Cas and Simeon, and Nique's crazy, pistol-toting ass, I thought as Amir dropped me.

I was on the floor gasping for air, staring at him.

"What the fuck is wrong with you?" Cas yelled.

"*Who* the fuck baby is that?" Amir yelled.

"Nigga, you tripping," Cas said as he shook his head.

"Come on, *Amina.* Tell me. Hell, tell us whose baby that really *is?"* Amir said as he hit me in the face with a balled up piece of paper.

I know this nigga didn't just hit me in the face, I thought as I unballed the paper. *This shit ain't right. It can't be right,* I thought as I studied the paper.

"Lie now, Bitch," Amir said as he walked away.

I waited until he was out of the church before I attempted to move. Simeon saw me struggling so he helped me up and we walked out of the church.

"Why me?" I looked to the sky and mouthed.

After all the drama at the church, I didn't feel like being around people so I powered my phone down and went home.

I took a long hot bath and popped a valium.

I crawled in my bed and was out. I woke up in the middle of the night and just laid there staring at the ceiling with so many thoughts going through my mind. *Where the hell is my baby?*

Amir

I know that wasn't the time or the place but fuck it. The shit had to be done. I gave that girl the world. I gave that bitch my heart and she fucked me royally. *How the fuck, matter fact, why the fuck would she do me like that? We could've worked that shit out. All she had to do was talk to me,* I thought as I inhaled the Kush smoke. I was riding through the hood thinking.

Cas kept calling, but I wasn't in the mood for company. I knew my nigga understood.

I was chain smoking blunts just riding when I ended up at the place I used to call home.

I sat there debating on if I should go in or not. After about an hour of sitting there, I said fuck it. I wasn't going in because I would've probably killed her for sure that time around.

I smashed out and went to Clappers. I needed to clear my mind.

I was drinking Patron straight out of the bottle trying to sort through the bullshit. The more I thought about it, the more I wanted to kill her and whoever the nigga was. I decided to put the bullshit to the side and enjoy all the ass clapping in my face.

Chapter 18

Enzo

Tonight must be my lucky night, I thought as I watched Amir living it up like he didn't have a care in the world.

"Yo, Has, you got your heater on you?" I inquired.

"I stay strapped. Why?" Hasaan asked while looking around the club.

I wasn't trying to keep yelling over the music because I knew those hoes' lips will get loose for the right price.

I just sat back and kept my eyes on that nigga. Hasaan finally peeped game. He was so lost in Cherry's ass that he didn't even realize the mistake he made.

"Yo, ain't that Amir over there wit that red bone? Nigga, we should do him right now," he said all hype.

I clinched my jaw and gave him a *nigga you just fucked up* look. *This simple ass nigga may have just fucked up my money with his big ass mouth. I have to get rid of this nigga, too. One weak link will break a whole chain,* I thought as I sat and watched Amir enjoy his last lap dance.

I didn't realize Cherry was gone until I saw her on the pole.

I hope that bitch don't run her mouth, I thought as I watched her make her pussy blow bubbles.

Amir

I was watching Persia pussy pop on my table, unaware that death was lurking.

She hopped off the table and started clapping her ass in my face. I made it rain on her. Then she started grinding on my dick.

"Damn, P, I know you gon' let me in tonight?" I whispered in her ear.

"Daddy, you know you don't have to ask. What time you coming thru?" she asked.

"We can leave *now*, ma," I said.

"Let me go get dressed and tip out for the night, daddy," she said as she walked away.

I watched her walk away as I finished my second bottle of Patron. I paid my tab and waited for Persia.

Enzo

"Aye, Persia, let me talk to you real quick," Has said as Persia walked by our table.

"Time is money. What do you want, Has?" she asked with an attitude.

"How does fifty stacks sound?" Has asked.

"It sounds like music to my ears, but I'm a *show me the money* type of bitch," she said with her hand on her hip.

"Yo, Maine, hand me ten," he said as he looked Persia in the eye.

I handed him ten stacks.

This nigga think he a boss. How the fuck he gon' just add her in the mix. For all he know, she can fuck us over, I thought as I butted into the conversation and said, "How bout we give you half now as down payment and the rest once you come thru for us?"

She looked between me and Has like she really had to think about it.

"Hell yea, I'm in. What you need?" she asked excitedly.

"I need you to get Amir alone and let us in. We have some unfinished business," I said.

"Give me your number. I will text you the location," she said.

I gave her Has's info and she went on about her business.

"Nigga, let's move," I said as I tapped Has.

We went to the car. I went to the trunk and grabbed my twin desert eagles and we waited. I wanted to put a bullet in Hasaan's head right then but I needed him.

He was still hype off Cherry, talking about how he was gonna fuck her and what not.

You would think this nigga never had pussy from a semi bad bitch before, I thought.

"Nigga, pay attention. He should be coming out any minute now," I said as I watched the door.

Amir

That bitch Cherry was putting on a mean ass show. I wanted to see if she could do that on the dick.

When Persia came out, I told her to holla at her girl and see if she was down to fuck tonight.

She came back talking about for the right price she'd be there. I guess she didn't know it was me. I don't pay for pussy but I played the game and told P to tell her okay.

"I'mma pull the car around, y'all should be out front by then," I said.

As soon as I stepped out the door, I was greeted by a hail of bullets.

Damn, why didn't I let Cas know where I was? Why did I leave my gun in the car? This nigga caught me slipping again, I thought.

I faintly heard screaming and footsteps. When I looked up, I saw Enzo's face. I looked him in the eyes, smiled a bloody smile, and I gurgled out, "*Fuck* you." Then everything went black.

Jermaine

"Naw, nigga, fuck you," I said.

I watched him take his last breath. I ran back to the car and dipped out.

"Nigga, we got him. We finally got him," Hasaan cheered.

I looked at that nigga like *no I got him* but I had to keep the peace for now. So I joined in with his little celebration.

Shit, I didn't get the connect. That's alright, I will get it tho. I have to get back in good with Mina, I thought as I pulled up at the spot.

I killed the engine, rolled some Cali Kush, and started plotting.

"Nigga, pass that shit," Hasaan said, bringing me out of my thoughts.

I passed him the blunt and we chopped it up. Then he hopped out.

I called Keta. "Have that pussy ready, I'm on my way," I said. I started my car and skirted off.

Persia

That spoiled little bitch thought her shit didn't stink. Well let's see how she survives now, I thought as I watched Amir get gunned down.

I could not stand my cousin. Call me jealous, I don't give a fuck. It's deeper than that. If it wasn't for that little bitch, my daddy would still be alive.

My revenge has only just begun, I thought as I watched people ducking and running.

Poor Amir was lying there just bleeding out. Thanks to him, I could take an early vacation. I walked away from the door and went out the back exit. Shit was about to get hot around here fast and I didn't want to be around.

Cason

I was on my way to Clappers. I needed to clear my mind. I called Simeon and Amir to see if they wanted roll with me but neither one of them niggas answered.

When I pulled up, police were everywhere. I slowly rode by to see if I could see anything.

"What the fuck? I know dat ain't my nigga," I yelled as I threw my car in park and hopped out.

"What the fuck happened? Who did this shit?" I screamed at the onlookers, but nobody said anything.

An officer walked over trying to calm me down, but I wasn't hearing that shit.

"Fuck out my face and do ya job, get my nigga to a hospital," I gritted.

He reached for his and I reached for mine. I didn't give a fuck. My nigga was laying there leaking and he was fucking with me.

His partner saw what was about to go down and quickly intervened.

"Officer Shaw, I need you to get some witness statements *now,*" his partner said.

"He was being disorderly."

"Shaw, I said *now. I got this,*" Detective Ross said.

He pulled me to the side. "Nigga, I'ma find out all that I can for you. You know that's my nigga, too."

"Man, if my nigga don't make it, I'ma turn this city upside down, cuz," I barked.

"Who could've done this, Cas? Help me so I can help us," Detective Ross said.

"Holla at me when you get off. I gotta call wifey and Amina," I said.

I walked away.

I know one of these hoes know something and if I find out they had a hand in this, I'ma blow this bitch out the ground, I thought as I dipped out shooting a bird at officer Shaw.

My first call was to Nique. Then I called Simeon and had him round up the crew and meet me at the hospital. When I got to the house, Nique was standing outside dressed in all black, looking like a goon.

I laughed and shook my head. *My baby is trained to go,* I thought as I watched her walk to the car. I didn't know what to say because next to me, that nigga was her heart.

I sat in the driveway with the engine idling, looking straight ahead because I would break if I looked at her.

"Baby, have you talked to Mina?" I asked lowly.

"No, I tried to call her but she must've turned her ringers off. Why what's goin' on?" she asked.

"It's Amir," I whispered.

"Cas w-w-what you mean? Where is he, Cas? Where's my cousin?" she asked nervously.

"He was shot. It didn't look good," I said as a lone tear ran down my cheek.

Nique wiped my tear away as I pulled out of the driveway. She turned the music up and we rode to Mina's.

Amina

I kept hearing a loud banging. I thought I was dreaming so I didn't move. The banging stopped, eventually. Then I heard glass shatter.

What the hell? I thought as I jumped up and grabbed my baby nine.

I quietly walked out of my room and tip-toed to the top of the steps, gun cocked and ready to shoot.

"Why the fuck didn't you bring your key? Now I gotta pay for this shit," Cas fussed.

"Nigga, you said get dressed. You didn't say for what. I thought I had to do some work," Nique said.

Nique and Cas fussed as he helped her through my living room window.

I flicked the light on and they had the nerve to be startled.

"What the hell are y'all doin'? Where is your key?" I asked.

"That doesn't matter right now. Just go get dressed. We gotta go," Nique said.

The seriousness in her voice let me know that whatever had happened wasn't good.

My first thought was *Amir.*

I hurried to get dressed while they boarded up my window. Then we left.

The ride was silent. When we pulled up to the hospital, my heart dropped.

I followed them out of the car. When we got inside, I saw Amir's mom, Ms. Cynthia. I knew it was Amir.

They filled me in on what happened, but I wasn't trying to hear that. I just wanted Amir to be okay.

Phoenix

Chapter 19

Jermaine

That nigga thought he was untouchable. He must didn't get the memo. A lil nigga done grew up. My guns bust just like his used to. I was feeling myself.

I just killed the head, now the body had to fall.

I swagged into Keta's house and she was naked on her knees by the door waiting for me like a bitch is supposed to be.

I patted her head as she slid my foot-long dick down her throat with ease. I beat her throat up until I came. She sucked me till I was hard again. I put her up against the wall and fucked her from the back in both holes. She was matching me stroke for stroke.

"*Ahhhh shit, Amir, Amir,*" she screamed out.

I know this hoe didn't just call me another nigga's name. I kept stroking that pussy because I was going to get my nut.

I fucked her with no mercy and when I was done, I threw her to the ground and pissed on her. "You lucky that's all I did, bitch. My name is Enzo, E-N-Z-O," I said as I walked out.

The Hospital
Cason

Damn, what the fuck I'ma do without my right hand? That nigga gotta make it. I was pacing the floor, waiting for good news. To pass time, everybody was telling stories about some shit Amir did, just trying to keep everybody's spirits up. Whoever did this shit wanted my nigga dead and they may be coming after me next.

"Yo, Simeon, let me holla at you real quick," I said.

"Get Keys on the phone and get me all the info on that nigga

Enzo and his family," I said.

I walked away. My gut was telling me that he was the one that did this shit, but I needed to be sure. I was about to take the streets by storm.

"Is there a Cason James present?" the nurse asked.

I walked over to her. She spoke in a hushed tone and led me back to talk to the doctor.

Amina

Look at these fake hoping for the best ass niggas. Sitting up here acting like they care when they couldn't give a fuck less.

Amir didn't fuck with half of these niggas outside of business, but they up here acting like shit sweet.

Truth be told, half these niggas here owe him money. Now that he's down, they're out of hiding.

They got me fucked up tho, I thought as I watched them chopping it up and shit.

"I'm sick of this shit," I said.

I got up to go confront these niggas.

"Why the fuck are y'all here? Amir didn't get down with y'all like that," I gritted, looking each one of them in their eyes.

"Quiet as it's kept, most of y'all niggas been hiding from him 'cause y'all owe him money. Now that he's down, y'all out of hiding, which means y'all got that money. So run that shit," I ordered with my hand out.

I wasn't trying to hear the bullshit they were trying to feed me. All I wanted to see was money in my hand and their backs as they walked out the fucking door.

I saw the mean mugs and I heard the mumbled threats and whatnot, but ask me if I gave a fuck. *Hell no,* I was just telling it like it was.

After my lil outburst, I apologized to Ms. Cynthia, but the shit had to and needed to be said.

Ms. Cynthia was cool about it. She understood where I was coming from.

Nique and I talked with her. But after a while, I tuned them out. My mind was on Amir.

I was wondering what the hell was taking the doctor so long to come talk to us. I felt like I was in the twilight zone. I had just buried my son and now his dad was fighting for his life.

I knelt down next to Ms. Cynthia and prayed with her while everybody else was reminiscing.

I wanted to tell them all to shut the hell up because they were talking like he was dead. I couldn't take it anymore, so I went outside to get some air.

"Mina, you alright?" Simeon asked.

"I'm just here right now. Thank you for checking on me," I said.

"I know you want to be alone, but I can't do that," Simeon said.

"Simeon, I don't need a fucking babysitter," I yelled.

Cason

I couldn't take not knowing what was going on, so I stepped outside to burn one and clear my mind.

"Why didn't you call me? Where the fuck was your vest?" I said out loud as I blew the Cali in the air.

"Yo, Keys, what's good?" I said.

"This nigga is a fucking ghost. nobody knows who he is or where he hang, but he getting crazy money in Indy, Tennessee,

Kentucky, and Georgia," Keys said.

"Then we are the Ghost Busters, nigga. Get some teams together and hit every spot he got," I gritted.

I ended the call and walked over to Mina and Simeon.

"Y'all good over here?" I asked.

"We good, I came to keep an eye on her," he said.

"I don't need a damn babysitter. Where the fuck were y'all when Amir was gunned down?" she yelled. Then she punched me in the chest.

I knew she was hurting just as bad as I was. I held her until she calmed down while Simeon went to go get Nique.

Once Nique was out there, me and Simeon went to discuss business.

Amina

"I thought this shit was over. Now I gotta look over my shoulder. Maybe AJ dying was a blessing. I couldn't raise him around all this, Nique," I said.

"I know this ain't a way to live, but this the hand we were dealt. We chose this life and AJ would've been protected from this madness," she said.

"They, whoever the hell *they* are, tried to kill him. *They* gunned him down like a fucking wild animal and left him to die," I said.

"They're goin' to pay for what they did," she said.

"What happens next, huh? What the fuck happens next? Is everything goin' to go back to normal? Is the pain going to go away? What if he don't make it, huh?" I yelled.

"He's a fighter. He gon' come out this shit stronger than ever," Nique said.

We cried and held each other.

After we got our emotions together, we smoked one. Then we went to the cafeteria.

"So what was that all about at the funeral?" Nique asked while eating a fry.

"Honestly, I have no idea. That really is his baby. You seen him. I don't know where the hell he got that test from," I said looking her in the eyes.

She sat there contemplating her next question for a while.

"Are you sure, Mina? Remember the night in Indy?" she asked.

I put my head down and said, "I wanted to forget that night. But I know we used protection and it didn't break."

"Even you said that it wasn't your baby. I thought it was just shock. But with what Amir said, now I'm not sure," Nique said.

I was thinking about what she said and my mind I didn't believe that was my baby. I didn't believe that God could be so cruel. But then my mind began to wonder, maybe she was right.

Phoenix

Chapter 20

Jermaine

This is like shooting fish in a fucking barrel, I thought as I watched Cas, his girl, the dread head, and Amina outside consoling each other.

I could've killed them all, but watching them suffer was too much fun.

I'ma take everything from that bitch ass nigga Cas. Then I'ma make him bleed too, I thought as I pulled off.

"Reem, is de plane ready?" I asked.

"Yea mon everyting ire," Reem said as he pulled off.

Cason

Dahlia was blowing my phone up, but I wasn't on her right now. I had to make sure my nigga was good.

I was about to go into the waiting area when I was stopped by the doctor. He told me that Amir's surgery was a success. But with the severity of his injuries, he wasn't out of the woods yet.

We finished up our conversation. I shook his hand and thanked him as I watched him walk into the waiting area to talk to everybody else. I said a silent prayer, thanking God for pulling him through. Then I walked into the waiting area smiling.

"Amir is a fighter. He sustained multiple gunshot wounds to his abdomen and chest area. He lost a lot of blood but we were able to stabilize him and remove the bullets. The next twenty four hours are very crucial. You will be able to visit with him briefly. I will send a nurse out to escort you to his room momentarily," the doctor said.

Ms. Cynthia was asking him questions. He answered them all. Then he made brief eye contact with me and left.

My head was in my hands. Nique was rubbing my back, trying to comfort me, and my phone was still going crazy.

How did I get myself into this shit? I thought as my phone started vibrating once again.

"Cason, could you come with me please?" Porsha, the nurse, asked.

Shit, not her again, I thought as I got up to go with her. I know Nique is burning a hole in my back.

This bitch better not be on some other shit. I followed her to a secluded hallway

"Yo, I don't know what you on but it ain't even like that, shorty. I love my girl and you ain't worth my happy home," I said as I continued to follow her.

"I just want to show you something. Then you can go back to your lil girlfriend," she said with a smirk as she pushed me into a room and closed the door.

I ain't gon lie my dick jumped a lil bit. I love that aggressive shit, but I couldn't do my girl like that.

"Look, shorty..." I started to say but I was cut off.

"Nigga, she ain't trying to fuck your scary ass," Amir said with a raspy laugh. I turned around, happy to see my nigga awake and talking.

"Nigga, we thought you were... nevamind that shit, I'm 'bout to go get ma dukes and them," I said.

I headed towards the door.

"Wait, let me holla at you real quick," Amir rasped as the nurse was fluffing his pillows.

I grabbed a chair and listened to him.

I wasn't feeling the way he wanted to handle things, but his mind was made up and I was down for the ride. I got myself together then I went to go get everybody.

Amir

I should've never let that nigga live. I broke the golden rule, never leave any witnesses. That hoe ass nigga think he gon get away wit this shit tho, I thought as I waited for Cas to bring everyone back to see me.

Everybody started coming in the room hugging me and all that stuff.

As I looked around the room, I couldn't tell who was real and who was fake.

Were these tears of joy that was alive, or were they tears of pain? Where the fuck is Amina? I thought as I scanned the room.

It was getting hard for me to breathe and my eyes were getting heavy. I looked into my mom's eyes as a single tear escaped. I never wanted to cause her any pain.

I didn't know who I could trust besides my family. *Where is Amina?* I thought again. It as if she read my mind, in walked my sunshine. I locked eyes with her. She looked so beautiful. I mouthed, "I love you." Then I closed my eyes. The machines were going crazy and the small room became chaotic. Doctors and nurses rushed in and shut off the machines.

Amina

"What are you doin'? Turn that back on. Save my baby!" Ms. Cynthia screamed.

"Time of death 6:15 pm," the doctor said.

"*Nooooo,* Lord, not my baby. Jesus, not my baby. What did you do, huh? What did you do?" Ms. Cynthia sobbed as she grabbed the doctor's lab coat.

I was in shock, numb. I couldn't believe he was gone. The room was overcome with emotions. Nique was lying next to Amir talking to him. Cas punched a hole in the wall, and poor Ms. Cynthia lost it. Simeon had to pull her off the doctor.

The walls felt like they were closing in on me. I had to get out of there, so I left and took a cab home. Once I got to my house, I went straight to the bar and poured me a drink. Hell, I grabbed the whole damn bottle and took it to the head.

"Why did you leave me, huh?" I said as sobs rocked my body.

"Amir, I'm sorry. I'm so sorry. Take care of our son. I love y'all," I said as I cried.

Cason

"Fuck," I yelled as I punched the wall.

I couldn't take watching the pain and heartache ma dukes and Nique were going through.

I stepped out in the hall to get myself together and to check on Ms. Cynthia.

After I made sure she was good, I asked Simeon to take her home so she could rest. Plus, I didn't want her to nut up on anybody else. I went back in the room to get Nique because the nurses needed to get Amir's body ready for the funeral home.

I walked into the room and picked her up.

I held her while they cleaned him up and the funeral home came in and took him. She tried to break free but I wouldn't let her go. Watching her hurt like that fucked me up. I held her tighter and told her to let it out. The next thing I knew, I was slapped.

Dominique

I know this is one of Amir's twisted ass jokes. He's going to wake up any minute now laughing and calling all of us soft, I thought.

"Amir, quit playing. This shit ain't funny. You know when you get up auntie is goin' to kick your ass for this," I said as tears streamed down my face.

I wanted him to get up so bad, but I knew in my heart he was gone. I laid there talking to him until Cas came and lifted me out of the bed. We sat in the chair. Amir looked so peaceful.

I was lying on Cas's chest. I thought I smelled perfume, but I dismissed it and kept watching Amir. I was cool until the men from the funeral home came in. I tried to get away from Cas and but he held me tighter.

"Amir, please get up, please. This ain't funny," I yelled.

I buried my face in Cas' neck and was met with a strong smell of perfume. *The nerve of this nigga,* I thought as I slapped him and ran down the hall.

"I can't believe this nigga," I mumbled to myself as I walked to the car.

I tried to call Mina but she wasn't answering. I sped up when I saw Cas approaching the car. I flipped him off and headed to the house to grab Mina's keys. Then I was going to check on her. I called Farrah and told her to meet me at Mina's. My phone was making all kinds of noise, so I powered it down and turned up my music.

Farrah

I had to put on my concerned cousin face when I really didn't give a fuck about what Amina was going through. Her ass deserved to feel some pain, shit.

I should have never told her about the game my daddy played with me when I was nine and she was seven. We would play it when my mom was sleep or at work. That was our special time.

One night over the weekend, Mina spent the night and my daddy said he wanted her to play with us.

We waited until my mom was asleep. Then we went down to the basement. I kissed my dad on the lips. Then he made me kiss her. She hesitated, but my dad threatened to whoop her so she let me kiss her. My dad pulled out his big magic wand. I loved playing with daddy's wand. He said that my touch cured his sickness and I didn't want my daddy to be sick.

I tried to tell Mina that, but she wouldn't touch it. She ran to wake my mom up and I ran to my room. I pretended to be sleep but I was listening. Mina told my mom what happened in the basement and then came to bed. I heard fighting then my dad came in my room he kissed my forehead. He quietly tipped toed out of the room. When I woke up, my dad was gone. Two weeks later, he was found dead in an alley. I knew it was her fault.

The sound of Nique's voice brought me back to reality.

I wanted to hang up on Dominique, but I agreed to meet her at Mina's house.

Hell, maybe I will see her fine ass man and give him some head in the bathroom while those hoes cry their eyes out, I thought as I searched for something to wear. It was sad that Amir was gone. I could've saved him that night, but seeing my favorite cousin fall from grace was worth more in my eyes. My only regret was I didn't get to fuck him before he died.

Cason

I know that bitch seen me coming to the car. Then she had the nerve to shoot me the bird tho. When I catch her ass, I'ma fuck her up, I thought as I pulled out my phone to call Simeon.

"Yo, come pick me up from the hospital. Nique flipped on me and dipped," I said to Simeon and ended the call.

While I waited for Simeon, I decided to return some of the calls I'd missed earlier, starting with the workers.

"Man, why the fuck Amir bitch bark on me like that, puttin' my business out there and shit? That shit wasn't cool, Cas. Had that been any other bitch I would've…" Smoke fumed.

I cut his ass off because I'd heard enough. I looked at my phone shaking my head. *I know this nigga didn't. he must've ate a hearty portion of Wheaties today*, I thought as I hung up the phone. *I'ma make an example out of this nigga tho.*

I called Wop and told him to round them niggas up and meet me at Casonique's.

Casonique's was an upscale boutique that sells one of a kind, exclusive outfits, shoes, and other shit these chicks be out here buying but for us. It was our headquarters. That was where it all started.

Once we started getting money, we gutted the place and fixed it up.

Man, if those walls could talk, my spirit wouldn't be free after I died.

To calm my nerves, I called Dahlia. But she was on some "leave ya girl, be wit me" type shit, so I quickly ended that call.

Shit, I had enough going on. I didn't have time to deal with that stupid shit. Finally, Simeon's ass pulled up. I told him to head to the store as I filled him in on what happened. I needed to release some of the tension and one or all of them niggas were perfect candidates to be my punching bag.

Amina

I had been lying on the floor in the fetal position, crying till I couldn't cry anymore. My phone had been ringing off the hook, so I decided to pull myself off the floor and turn on some music to drown it out. Since I was up, I decided to take a shower and clear my mind.

I was trying to figure out why Cas was talking to the doctor.

Did he set Amir up? I thought as the water rained down on me.

"Mina, ma, are you alright?" Nique said as she stuck her head through the bathroom door.

"Yea, I'm good. I will be out in a minute," I replied.

I really wasn't in the mood for company but I didn't want to be alone either. I stayed in the shower until the water got cold. Then I got out, put on some clothes, and rolled one.

"How you holding up, boo?" I asked as I passed her the blunt and gave her a hug.

"I can't believe that he's gone. I keep wanting this to be one of his twisted ass jokes," Nique said

A tear rolled down her cheek. I knew this was going to be super hard for her to deal with.

I made my mind up to be strong for both of us as I made us a drink.

"I called Farrah. She should be on her way. Let's order some food, or you cook, because I am hungrier than a hostage," Nique said.

"When ain't your ass hungry? Let me find out you pregnant," I said with a giggle.

I walked to the kitchen. Everything was frozen so I decided to order pizza, wings, and some Chinese food.

"Girl, I think Cas fucking somebody else," she said.

"Yea, right. How you know?" I asked.

"I'm dead ass. The nigga was trying to comfort me at the hospital and smelled just like that bitch. I slapped the shit outta him and left," Nique said. she took a pull on the blunt.

"I never would've thought he would step out on you. I'm sorry you're going thru that," I said as I rubbed her back.

I wonder if that's why he wasn't with Amir, I thought as the doorbell rang. I grabbed my purse because I thought it was the food, but it was just Farrah.

"Hey, cousin." I smiled as I embraced her.

Farrah

I swear I wanted to punch her in the face but I plastered a fake smile on my face and hugged her back.

I waltzed past her into the house and found Dominique turning a bottle of tequila up.

"Look at this drunk bitch," I said to myself as I removed my shades.

The house was nice. Since Mina and Nique were in the family room, located in the back of the house, I took myself on a tour.

I walked around the house looking at all the pictures of Amir. I slipped a pic of him with his shirt off in my bag. Then I wandered off to their room to see what other treasures I could find. I was rambling through her nightstand when I came across a naked pic of him. I was just about to swipe it, but the doorbell rang and scared me so I closed the drawer. But I made a mental note to go back for that pic later as I quietly exited their room.

"The foods here ladies," I announced as I opened the door and greeted the delivery girl.

She was thick as fuck. I flirted a little but she was shy. I saw the look of relief on her face when Amina appeared to pay her.

"Girl, leave her alone before she run off wit our food," Amina said as she playfully pushed me out of the way.

"I love 'em shy," I said as I winked and walked away.

I wonder where Cason's fine ass is, I thought as I walked back into the house. I sat on the couch next to Dominique and decided to pick her brain. "Honey, you've been knocking back those drinks pretty fast. Slow down, lush," I said as I bounced down next to her.

"Seriously tho, I know this is hard for you and if you ever need anything, I'm just a phone call away," I said.

"My cousin is gone forever. Cason is cheating on me. *Me.* Girl, I'm sorry. It's just a lot goin' on with me, but I will keep that in mind. Thank you," Nique said as she hugged me.

"It's okay, girl, that's what I'm here for," I said as I rubbed her back.

Damn, so Cason ain't gon' be here. I would say this was a wasted trip. But with the pics and this little bit of information, I'm glad I came, I thought as I grabbed my glass and made a toast to myself.

Amina

"I think I ordered too much food," I said to myself.

I saw that Farrah and Nique were having a moment, so I took the food in the kitchen and made my plate.

"The food is on the counter and y'all know where the plates are," I said as I sat down.

As I looked around, all I saw was Amir looking at me.

I wanted him to walk through that door so bad. I suddenly lost my appetite. I didn't want to be bring them down so I excused myself and went to lay down.

I thought about all the good times we shared and all the things we were supposed to do. Even after he damn near choked me to death, I still loved that man.

If he was to walk in the door right now, it would be like nothing ever happened.

My neck was still a little sore, too. That nigga had the death grip on me. I giggled as I gently rubbed my neck.

"Mina, are you okay?" Farrah asked as she walked into my room and lay next to me.

"I'm alright. I just needed a moment and I didn't want to bring y'all down."

"It's okay to mourn. We are mourning, too. You are more than a cousin to me, you are my sister and your pain is mine. Do you want me to stay the night?" Farrah asked.

"No, I know you have stuff to do. I will be alright," I said.

"Clappers will survive one night without me, boo. If you need me to stay, I will stay. But I'm giving you the heads up, I sleep naked," Farrah said trying to lighten the mood.

"You are so silly. Go 'head and go to work. Nique will be here," I said.

"Well I'ma get out of here. Call me if you need me. I love you, Mina Beena," she said as we air kissed. Then she breezed out of my room.

Phoenix

Chapter 21

Cason

"Simeon, roll up a couple and let's politic for a minute," I said to Simeon as we pulled up in the back of the store.

"What's goin' on wit cha?" Simeon asked as he broke down the weed.

"Shit, nigga, everything. This shit wit Amir got me way past heated. I want to body anybody that ever beefed wit us cause I don't know who this Enzo nigga is, feel me?" I said.

"I feel you. I feel you. What's this meeting about?" Simeon said between tokes.

"That slow to pay, hide and go seek ass nigga, Smoke, called me crying 'bout how Mina barked on him and shit," I said.

"That nigga a bitch. Yo, nigga, she went hard on them niggas. It wasn't just him tho. I was about to say something but I felt like they needed to hear that shit and she was holding her own. Shit was funny to me," Simeon said.

"The nigga, Smoke, violated in a major way, so him and anybody else that's siding with him is 'bout to learn a very valuable lesson," I said with a sinister smile as I took the last pull on the blunt.

When we got inside, niggas were sitting around gossiping like bitches. They didn't even notice us in the room.

"Man, fuck Amir and the money I owe him. That nigga dead and so is my debt. But his bitch, *I'ma* see her ass tho. I'ma show her what she supposed to do wit all that mouth," Debo said as a few niggas dapped him up and laughed with him.

I was seeing red at that point, but I held it together for the moment.

"Let me in on the joke. A nigga could use a good laugh right about now," I said, making my presence known. Them niggas looked like they could've shit a brick. I didn't stand around for the clowns to entertain me. Hell, they probably started talking about me when I walked away. But I'ma get the last laugh. I always do.

"I gathered y'all here today because it has come to my attention that some of you are in your feelings 'bout some shit that happened at the hospital," I said as I stood before them. I loved having power like that.

"Man, that bitch didn't have to put us on blast like that! I know what the fuck I owe. I know who run shit. I had the money, but I wasn't giving it to that bitch," Smoke said as the niggas she called out cosigned with him.

They gassed that nigga's head up, had him feeling like he was the boss and shit. So I let him have his moment.

I sat there with my head tilted, smirking and listening to this nigga go on with his little temper tantrum.

"Are you done, *boss*?" I asked sarcastically.

"My fault, man, that shit pissed me off tho. You can have the floor back," Smoke said as he took his seat.

I looked that nigga dead in his eyes as I spoke. "So the fuck what *she* don't run shit. When her nigga is down, *she* is his voice. And so what she exposed y'all. The shit needed to be said. Fuck all that tho. You said you got that money, so run it," I yelled as I banged on the table.

"Well, see, my baby moms had to..." Smoke said.

"*Fuck ya baby moms, nigga.* Run me that mafucking paper, bitch," I spoke through clenched teeth as I walked up on that nigga.

"I ain't got it Cas," Smoke whispered.

"Speak up, bitch. You had all that mouth a few minutes ago. Speak up now, bitch," I gritted.

"I don't have it on me, but when..." Smoke stammered.

"Fuck that, hoe ass nigga. You in here talking big boy like you on *your* shit. Now you trying to hit me with the bullshit," I said as I shot him in the head.

"Run me my mafucking money and get the fuck outta here. Oh yea, if y'all niggas in your feelings 'bout this shit, or anything else for that matter, y'all niggas know where to find me. And trust I stay ready, so bring ya A game. This meeting is over. Aye, Debo, let me holla at cha real quick," I said as I lit a blunt.

"What's up, Cas?" Debo said nervously.

I watched him as I inhaled the blunt, blowing the smoke out of my nostrils.

"You seem a lil nervous, nigga, calm down. Here, you wanna hit this?" I asked him as I offered him the blunt.

"I'm good, my nigga. Sorry to hear about Amir. He was a good dude," he said trying to sound as sincere as possible.

"Ya shit was short ten stacks. I'm in a good mood so you got till ten tonight to have my money, and don't make me have to come find you. Be easy, lil nigga," I said as I put my blunt out and pulled out my phone.

He hesitated like he had something to say but decided to bite his tongue and leave.

I thought about calling Nique, but I still needed to blow off some steam.

"Yo, Simeon, let's go to Clappers," I said as I got up and headed for the door.

Simeon

167

"Yo, nigga, I ain't ya fucking driver. I got some shit to do. I will drop you by ya crib so you can get ya whip and do you," I said.

Them other niggas catered to him, but not me. Fuck I look like?

"A'ight, nigga, that's cool. Calm down," Cas said with a laugh.

I dropped him off and headed to my house. I had been trying to figure out what my next move was going to be. A part of me was feeling Mina. *Maybe when this is all over, she will be my wifey*, I thought as I called Reem.

"Tell the boss they're still chasing a ghost," I said. I ended the call, and then called Ya-Ya.

"Wat up, Ya-Ya? How's the baby?" I asked.

"When are you comin' to get this little fucker? All he does is cry. Maybe my sister had the right idea," fumed Ya-Ya.

"Bitch, I will get there when I fucking get there. You just do what the fuck I'm paying you to do before you have to bury that slut ass sista of yours," I calmly stated as I ended the call

Mafuckas gon' stop thinking I'm a soft ass nigga. I think I will go to Clappers tonight. Nothing beats the cross like a double cross, I thought as I laid my clothes out, and then got in the shower.

I was in the shower humming a tune. I was in such a good mood.

Amir and Cason are some real ass niggas. They're good people, but I want to be the boss not a worker. I want the money and the power that comes with it. I don't give a fuck about respect. I want these streets to fear me like they fear God. I'm far from a broke ass nigga. I'm just tired of working for it. I want somebody to work for me and bring me that long paper. This short shit ain't getting it no more, I thought as the water rained down on me.

I was feeling myself and I knew once I hit the door, them hoes were gon' feel me too. *But tonight I'm on a mission for one hoe in particular,* I thought as I grabbed my keys and dipped out. I called Cas from the car and told him I was on my way.

Phoenix

Chapter 22

Clappers
Simeon

"I am *that* nigga. My girl need to understand that. These hoes come wit the territory. I love her and would never put another bitch before her, but sometimes I just want to fuck without all the emotions. Ya feel me, nigga?" Cas slurred.

"Nigga, sit your drunk ass down. If Nique heard you talking this bullshit, she would beat your ass. Yea, you that nigga alright," I laughed.

"You right. You right. Nique would kick my ass. She was down wit a nigga when all I had was lint in my pockets. Nigga, she's my world and I fucked up, but I'ma dwell on that shit later. Right now, I'ma enjoy these hoes," Cas boasted while looking at a butter pecan cutie with a lot of ass.

That nigga sounded ridiculous. That shit may have been cool when we were younger, but having all them bitches now was played out. A nigga in this crazy ass game would love to have a woman like Nique at home. Don't get me wrong, by no means am I a saint. I have had my share of bitches, but I never stepped out on my girl when I had one. But hey, to each its own.

"What's up, Cherry? Bring me a bottle of Patron and Ciroc," I said.

"Okay, sexy, holla at me before you leave," she said with a wink as she walked away.

"Bitch, why was you all up in Simeon face like that?" Persia harshly whispered.

"Hoe, I was working. Fuck is wrong with you?" Cherry asked.

"Yea okay, let me find out," Persia said as she flipped her hair and walked away.

Cason

Clappers was at capacity and I was on point. money was in the building tonight. I watched these niggas pop bottle after bottle wondering if one of them set my nigga up.

It looked like they were celebrating my nigga's demise. A few niggas came by my table and expressed their sympathies. I didn't feel the sincerity in their words. I thanked them and they kept it moving. I didn't trust none of those niggas.

I was snapped out of my thoughts when Persia walked up and clapped her ass in my face.

"Damn," I whispered as I caught a glimpse of her fat ass pussy.

My dick jumped when she went down and kissed it through my jeans. She winked at me as she did her thang.

I made it rain on her head. Then she got up and gave me a lil show. I peeped Simeon watching me. I saw the jealousy in his eyes.

In that moment he wished he was me. *I might let him get my leftovers*, I thought as I smirked at him and mouthed, "I'm that nigga."

He just shook his head, knocked a shot back, and took a pull on the blunt. He passed it to me and I took a few pulls in between chopping it up with a few niggas. I was cool while Persia did her thing.

I wanted to call Nique but my ego wouldn't let me. I knew I'd fucked up and being at the strip club wasn't making things better.

Simeon

This nigga is really feeling himself right now. The way he moving, I'm starting to think he had a hand in sending Amir home and not Enzo, I thought as I watched Cas.

"Ayo, Cherry bomb, I'm 'bout to buy the bar out, so tell these niggas to save their money," Cas slurred.

"Yo, read this," I said as I passed Cas the note Cherry gave me.

"Fuck you get this from?" Cas asked.

"Somebody sent it to me with a drink," I said. I sobered up real quick. *So one of these hoes know who did it,* I thought as I looked around at all of the strippers in the room.

"I'ma meet with the hoe and see what she talking 'bout. Who gave you the drink?" Cas asked.

"Nigga, I don't know. The shit was on the table by my fresh drink. I peeped the scene after I read it, but I didn't see anything out of the ordinary," I said.

Xstasy walked up just as we finished our conversation.

"You want lap dance, sexy?" she asked me.

"Have a seat, baby. What you drinking?" I asked Xstasy.

She had a shocked look on her face when she responded. I knew she was working, so I made sure she was compensated for her time as I got to know her.

Since Cas was handling that situation, it gave me time to work on Xstasy.

"Go get your stuff, you're goin with me," I whispered in Xstasy's ear.

She smiled and went to do as she was told.

"Nigga, you straight? Cause I'm 'bout to dip," I asked Cas.

"Yea, I'm good. Go do your thang, nigga. I will let you know what happen," Cas said I gave him some dap then went to get Xstasy.

Cason

I went to the dressing room, but I didn't see anybody. I waited a little bit longer, but nobody ever came. I was pissed because somebody was playing games, so I made my way to the exit.

When I got to my car, Persia was leaning up against my door. I eased her out of the way. Then I got in and pulled out my phone to call Nique.

Persia opened my door, pulled my dick out, and gave me the best head I ever had. If I didn't know any better, I would've thought that hoe didn't have any teeth. She was deep throating my shit with no problems. I was trying to watch, but the shit was feeling so damn good that I leaned my head back, closed my eyes, and dropped the phone.

"*Ahhhhhh Shitttttttttt,*" I moaned.

Persia

"I knew I couldn't trust your ass," I said as I choked Cherry and pushed her into the employee bathroom.

I gripped tighter until I felt her stop struggling. I let her body hit the ground. Then I cut her tongue out and went to tip out for the night.

I peeped Cas coming from the back looking pissed.

I knew why he was mad and I knew exactly how to calm him down. I slipped out the side door and went to wait for him by his car.

When I saw Cas come out the club, I got wet instantly. If I was wearing panties, they would've been soaked. He pushed me out of the way and got in his ride. Since he didn't pull off, I figured I wanted to see what was up.

I opened his door and started sucking his dick. I didn't give a fuck about him being on the phone, *fuck* Nique.

If she was handling her business, her man wouldn't be letting me suck his dick right now.

He was so lost in my amazing head skills that he forgot all about his precious wifey and dropped the phone. So I decided to show out.

I started moaning and slurping loudly on his dick, making sure she heard it.

"Give me that nut, daddy," I said right before I took his dick all the way down my throat, clenching my throat muscles and humming at the same time, which caused him to moan loudly. He nutted all down my throat. I savored the flavor for a lil bit, then I swallowed it all and hit the end button on his phone.

"Here, you dropped this," I said as I handed him his phone.

I walked away and hopped in my truck, confidently knowing that he would be calling for my A-1 head game soon, real soon.

Phoenix

Chapter 23

Amina's House
Dominique

How could he do this to me? Am I not enough woman for him? I wonder if he is with her right now, I questioned myself as I lay on the floor staring at the ceiling. I wanted to call him and listen to his background just to see if he was with her.

I knew that would be childish but I was not the only woman who had done a background noise check call.

I was missing him terribly. Maybe I was tripping for nothing. Maybe it was my aunt's perfume, or Mina's, I concluded as I grabbed my phone to call him. It just rang and rang, which pissed me off all over again. I felt the urge to throw up, so I quickly got up off the floor and ran to the bathroom.

"I'm never drinking again," I moaned as I kept throwing up.

"Nique, you alright?" Mina asked as she held my hair back for me.

"Mmmmm hmmmm, I'm never drinking again," I said as everything I had eaten hit the toilet.

She held my hair and rubbed my back until I was done. I dry heaved for about two minutes. Then I lay on the bathroom floor.

"I love you, Minnnnna. We gon' be a'ightttt, ya know?" I slurred.

"I love you, too, girl," she said as she helped me up.

She laid me down in the guest room, put a bucket by the bed, and walked out.

Amina

Phoenix

After I made sure Nique was good, I went to lie down. I closed my eyes and tried to go to sleep but thoughts of Amir invaded my mind. I could smell his cologne. I could feel his arms around me.

"Daddy, I'ma find out who did this shit. I'ma make 'em pay," I said out loud.

I was just drifting off to sleep when my phone started ringing. Who the fuck, ughhhh?

"Hello," I answered angrily.

"Hey, baby, you miss daddy?" Maine asked.

"Really, *Jermaine,* I'm too beat for this bullshit. Your ass been out of sight. Now you calling me at two in the fuckin' morning. I have too much goin' to deal with this. So if you trying to get your dick wet, you called the wrong number," I said with an attitude.

"Damn, baby, I deserve that. I know I haven't been there. I've been handling some business. I'm sorry I should've called sooner but..." Maine was trying to say but I cut him off.

"Nigga, cut the bullshit. You know what, I've wasted enough of my breath on you. Goodnight," I spoke through clenched teeth and hung the phone.

Nigga got some nerve calling me, I huffed as I fluffed my pillow.

My text alert went off. I wasn't going to read it but I wanted to see if his thumbs spoke bullshit, too.

Unknown: *You have a couple snakes in your grass. Things aren't what they seem.*

I was lost. There wasn't a number for me to text back. I chalked it up as somebody had texted the wrong number.

I tried to go back to sleep but I couldn't, so I rolled one and thought about what the fuck I was going to do with Amir gone.

Ms. Cynthia was cool but I knew she gon' be trying to put my ass out before his body was warm in the ground. So I was planning to beat her to the punch.

I took another pull on the blunt. *Why the fuck was Cas so chummy wit the doctor? Where the hell was he when the shit went down? They were like brothers, jumped into this shit together, split everything down the middle. They were equal so why did he do it?* Then I thought about the text and grabbed my phone. I reread the message, feeling like maybe this was meant for me.

My mind was all over the place.

I finished my blunt. Then I peeked in on Nique. Then I stopped in the nursery. I sat in the rocking chair holding AJ's blanket.

The game was cold, the streets didn't love nobody, and I was mad as hell at God. The more I sat there, the more I became furious. I refused to cry anymore so I went to the basement, grabbed some boxes, and went to pack up his room. I was on a rampage. I even started packing my stuff.

I packed all my clothes and a few pictures I wanted of Amir.

The rest of this shit his mama can deal with, I thought as I taped up the last box.

When I was done packing, my stomach was growling. so I went to make a bowl of Applejacks and search for a moving truck and storage unit.

"What's with all the boxes?" Nique asked.

"Spring cleaning," I said dryly as I took another bite of my cereal.

I could feel Nique staring at me but I didn't give a fuck, nor was I about to acknowledge her presence

I got up, emptied my bowl, tossed it in the dishwasher, and went to go take a shower.

They probably set my nigga up and she over here faking like he cheating on her.

Amir and Cas were like peas in a pod. If you saw one, you saw the other. And if you didn't, trust and believe he wasn't far behind.

He probably sent her over here to see where my head was, to see if I figured out that they had a hand in this shit. They're going to feel my pain.

It was late but I wasn't sleepy, so I surfed the net looking for jobs and apartments.

I had my headphones on and the world tuned out. I felt my phone vibrate. It was another message from Anonymous. This one was a picture of a sleeping baby that vaguely reminded me of Amir.

I became hot with anger. *If this is one of Amir's hoes, I swear I'ma revive him and kill 'em again. A baby?*

"A *fucking* baby, Amir? This can't be my life right now," I yelled as tears threatened to fall from my eyes.

I tried my hardest to hold them back, but looking at that baby broke me down. As I cried, I vowed that those would be the last tears I shed for my baby and the nigga that walked all over my heart. I turned my music up and let the bass take me away.

Jermaine
I felt a little bad about how I did Keta. but that bitch violated and she needed to be taught a lesson.

As for Mina, I had to distance myself because I knew she was probably mourning over that hoe ass nigga Amir. I didn't want to hear that shit. Fuck that hoe ass nigga. See, Amir and his little crew of bitches thought they were untouchable.

They thought every nigga in the tristate area was scared of

them. But I wasn't and neither was my brother, Diablo.

Diablo used to serve them young niggas, but he got over on them.

Them niggas were from outta town, getting money in the Nap and they were getting love from niggas that ran in Diablo's circle. He felt slighted because Amir and his crew wasn't on their level. As far as he was concerned, they shouldn't have been able to pop bottles or have the same choice of bitches they had.

My crew was out there on the corner doing the same shit they were doing. I was his little brother and I could barely hang with him, *so* what the fuck made these niggas so special.

He was jealous that the young niggas got more respect than he did. He was the mafucking man. They were peons getting money in his city. They didn't deserve that type of respect.

The more he taxed them, the harder they worked. They expanded their operation in the Nap, in Cleveland, and even started making plans to branch out to the Ville.

He decided to fleece them. He sold them six keys of flour and two uncut keys.

In his mind, the young niggas would lose their clout, take the loss, and go running back to Cleveland.

They went back to Cleveland for a while to lay low and plan.

Diablo thought he had nothing to worry about. I tried to tell him to watch his back, but he felt like he was untouchable and they wouldn't try him because he had an army behind him.

Long story short, them niggas ran up in his shit while we were chillin' and laid him and five of his top workers out.

I would've died that day too had I not been in the bathroom. I peeked out the door and caught a glimpse of Amir as he was coming out of Diablo's work room with four bags.

I knew them niggas didn't plan on leaving any witnesses because they didn't have on any masks.

I would never forget his face and I vowed to make him pay.

At first, I was just going to fuck Amina to get back at him. But I started feeling the bitch, so that plan went out the window.

Then there was Keta. She was cool, gave me some valuable jewels about his spots and his crew, but she caught feelings for a nigga. I wasn't with that. I mean her pussy was good and her head was fire, but she wasn't wifey material, especially after she called out that nigga name while I was in it. She had served her purpose.

San Juan has been nice, the bitches have been all over a nigga, but I'm missing Mina. I know she probably pissed at me. I'ma send her some tickets to make up for my absence.

Dominique

I wonder what's up with Mina, I thought as I made me a cup of coffee.

I would still be sleep but all the noise she was making woke me up. I stood in the kitchen willing my head to stop pounding but I think that only made it worse, so I grabbed my coffee and a water. Then I went to go lay back down.

"*Shit.* What the hell?" I yelped as I hit my baby toe on a box.

As I looked around, I noticed more boxes. I figured she was feeling lonely and pulled out some old things of Amir's so I just limped back to go lay down.

My indicator light was flashing, letting me know I had a missed call and a message from Cas.

He usually doesn't do voicemails so I was interested in hearing what he had to say. I sat there in shock as I listened to *my* man get his dick sucked. I could tell he was enjoying it by the sound of his moans. Some hoe was going in on *my* man's dick and he didn't even to stop her.

I listened closely, trying to catch her voice, but I couldn't focus. All I heard was him enjoying that hoe's mouth.

To say I as mad was an understatement. I was seeing red. I couldn't believe he would do me like this after all we'd been through.

I laid there silently crying, thinking about what my next move would be. I loved him but I loved me more. The fact that he decided to go fuck somebody else let me know that he didn't give two fucks about me.

Ironically, my phone started ringing. It was Cason. I looked at the screen and laughed as I hit the reject button. His constant calling back to back lulled me to sleep.

Simeon

I took Xstasy to one of my spots so I could give her some one on one attention. When we got to my house, she was looking around in awe.

"Take a look around and make yourself at home. I'ma go get breakfast started, baby," I said as I kissed her on the cheek. She blushed and went to go look around.

I turned on some music and started cooking. Xstasy still hadn't come back to the kitchen, so I put our plates in the oven to keep them warm and I went to go find her.

I didn't have to search long. I found her in the bathroom enjoying a bubble bath. She looked so peaceful I didn't want to wake her. I grabbed a sponge and started washing her feet and legs. She woke up and looked at me with admiration.

"Stand up, ma," I said.

She did as I told her. I washed the rest of her body and rinsed her off.

Her pussy looked so damn appetizing. I wanted to dive in but I was being a gentleman. I gave her my robe to put on and led her downstairs to the dining room.

"What's your real name, baby, cause I can't introduce you to my mom wit your stage name?" I said.

"My name is Marketa but everybody calls me Keta," she blushed.

I grabbed her hand and kissed it before I replied, "That is a beautiful name for a beautiful woman. Tell me about yourself."

I knew I was laying it on thick but she was eating that shit up.

"Why are you doin' all this for me? You didn't have to do this to fuck. I would've given you the pussy without all this," Keta said.

I looked her into her eyes as I spoke.

"Why not you? I don't want to fuck. I want to get to know you and I know I didn't have to but I wanted to do this," I said.

She insisted on doing the dishes, but I wouldn't let her. I grabbed her hand and led her to my room, where I laid her down and gave her a full body massage.

She was so relaxed she fell asleep. As she slept, I took some pictures of us and sent them to Ya-Ya so she would know just how serious I was.

Chapter 24

Amina

I was startled out of my sleep by my ringing phone.

"*What?*" I angrily answered the phone.

"Baby, don't hang up, just listen. there are two tickets to San Juan waiting for you. You don't have to leave today and you can bring whoever you want. I'm sorry and I love you," Maine said.

I just ended the call. I have to get my number changed.

"I hope Nique ass is gone," I said to myself as I threw the covers off.

Damn, I'm getting a late start, but it's better late than never, I thought as I got myself together.

When I stepped out of my room, I had a new attitude.

I might just take Maine up on that trip, I thought as I grabbed a few small boxes and left.

I went riding around looking for places. I saw a few that caught my eye, but I needed to find something more affordable for the time being. I rode around for a few more hours, looking at places. then I went to get a storage unit and reserve a truck.

Once that was done, I called Farrah.

"Hey, hoe, you hungry?" I asked when she answered.

"It takes one to know one. I could eat. Where you want to go?" Farrah said.

"Meet me at Shirley's. I'm in the mood for something smothered," I said.

"Give me fifteen minutes and I will be there," Farrah said.

"Okay, see you in a minute," I said.

As soon as I ended my call, Nique was calling. I hit the ignore button.

Then a text came through. It was another picture of that baby. But this time he was staring at the camera grinning in the arms of a toffee colored woman.

I couldn't see her whole face because of the way the picture was cropped. My blood was boiling. this scary bitch was getting on my nerves. I wasn't about to deal with baby mama drama.

I didn't have to when he was alive and I damn sure ain't 'bout to start after his death.

Farrah

I sat there for a moment, replaying my night and reminiscing about the feel of Cas' dick down my throat.

I can't wait until next time. I'ma make him forget all about Nique and any other bitch he fucking, I thought.

I got up and started getting ready. I knew I told Mina fifteen minutes, but she knows that was an hour my time. While I was in my closet, I thought about how much I was going to Miss Cherry's amazing head skills. That girl knew what to do with her mouth. *Damn, I'ma miss that shit.*

I told her that what we had to do wasn't for the faint of heart.

I loved Amir but he wasn't my nigga. I feel bad that I ushered him to his death, but we all gotta go sometime, some sooner than others, I thought as I called Has.

"You know I cleaned up your mess so I expect a nice deposit to be made in my account before the end of business today," I demanded.

"*Bitch,* that was your mess. You saved your own life. I'm not giving you shit else," Hasaan barked, then ended the call.

That nigga had some nerve. He was gon' pay me or join

Cherry.

I know Mina is cussing me out, I thought as I got in the shower. Once I was fresh and dressed, I headed over to Shirley's.

Dominique

I woke up to an empty house and over fifty missed calls from Cas.

I wasn't ready to talk to him. But the sooner I got it out of the way, the better. I tried to call Mina but her phone just rang so I showered and went to check on my shop. When I got to the shop, I received a warm welcome and condolences. I told the ladies that I had come for a pick me up and they started filling me in on what had been going on. I was enjoying myself until Cason walked in.

"Let me holla at you real quick," he said.

"Excuse me, ladies. How may I help you, Mr. James?" I asked.

"Can we go somewhere to talk?" he asked.

"My office is just fine. Hurry up and say what you have to say and be on your way. I have a business to run," I stated as I walked into my office.

He closed the door and said, "I fucked up. I let some hoe suck my dick last night."

"Is that all, baby?" I asked with a smirk on my face.

"Nique, I didn't mean for you to hear it or for it to happen. I was calling…"

I held up my hand to stop him from talking.

"You didn't even try to stop her, nor did you have the decency to hang up the phone. *You* let this bitch suck your dick," I yelled as I slammed my hand down on the desk repeatedly.

"Is that whose perfume I smelled on you at the hospital? Did you fuck that nurse, too? You know what, I don't give a fuck.

Cason James, you do *you* and I'ma do *me* 'cause you have no respect for me or our relationship, so why the fuck should I?" I spoke through gritted teeth. "You know what, don't say shit else to me. Get *the* fuck out of *my* office," I calmly stated.

I saw him flexing his jaw. I knew he was pissed, so was I.

"Dominique I'm goin' to excuse that hot shit you talking. I know you're hurt and pissed off. If you ever in your mafucking life entertain the idea of another nigga, I will kill *you* and that *nigga.* That's a mafucking promise. You better fix ya attitude before we cross paths again," he casually spoke as he walked towards the door, "Oh and, baby, have a good day. I love you," he said, then he walked out the door.

I screamed and threw the picture of us at the door. *Thank god my office is soundproof,* I thought as I cleaned up my mess.

I knew those bloodhounds picked up on the tension as soon as he walked in. I wasn't about to go out there and face all the questions, so I stayed in my office and got some much needed paperwork done.

It was five o'clock when I took a break. I made the reservations at Sommeil and tried to call Mina. She still wasn't answering. I didn't have time to worry about why or what she was going through, I had problems of my own to deal with. I figured she would come around when she was out of her feelings. I gathered my things, told the ladies to lock up, and I left.

Shirley's
Amina

After sitting there for over an hour, a table was finally available. I followed the hostess. Once I was seated, I pulled out my phone to call Farrah. But I saw her walk in, so I put my phone away and studied the menu.

"Darling, darling, sorry for my tardiness, but you know beauty takes time," she said as we air kissed each other's cheeks. After our dramatic performance, we cracked up laughing.

"Sit down wit your silly ass," I said with a giggle as she took her seat.

Men were eye fucking my cousin and women were giving her the stank face. Farrah exuded sex no matter what she had on, and today was no different. Even though she was dressed down today, she still turned heads.

"So to what do I owe the pleasure of dining with you on this beautiful Saturday afternoon?" she asked.

"What has you so bubbly today, or should I ask who?" I asked with my brow arched.

"Girl, I had a good night at work, a very good night," she said.

"Speaking of work, I need you to get ya girl on," I said as I took a sip of my drink.

I watched Farrah as she thought about what I said.

"Girl, the dick I had last night would make me change my ways. It was long and just the right thickness, and his nut was so sweet, mmmm," she said as she licked her lips.

I giggled and took another sip of my drink

"I'm serious, Farrah, I need to make some money fast."

"Mina, you don't need money that bad. What's this really about 'cause that life ain't for you?" Farrah said as the waiter placed our food on the table.

As soon as the waiter was out of ear shot, I gave Farrah a piece of my mind.

"I am so fucking tired of people telling me what ain't for me. This is my fuckin' life. I know what I can and can't fucking handle," I said.

I gathered my bags and threw a Benji on the table before I walked out. Farrah sat at the table for a little bit before she came out to talk to me. She came out just in time.

"Mina. Mina, wait. I know it's your life. I'm just trying to protect you. If you sure that's what you want, then I will hook you up," Farrah said.

I looked at her for moment before I spoke.

"Farrah, I'm sorry I snapped at you. It's just so much going on. My mind is all fucked up right now, but I'm sure this is what I want," I said. then I gave her a hug.

"Mina, what's goin' on?" she asked.

"Too damn much. I will fill you in another day. So when do I start?" I asked.

"Come in with me tonight and I will talk to Chino for you. You know I got your back. I love you, girl," she said.

"I love you, too. I will see you tonight," I said as I got in my car to leave.

I forgot to tell Farrah about the trip. I will tell her at the club tonight, I thought as I turned into my driveway.

When I walked into the house, I saw the light on my answering machine blinking so I clicked play and continued to put my things away. The message was from Ms. Cynthia, letting me know that Amir's funeral would be on Friday. I made a mental note of it and erased the message. Then I went to get prepared for tonight.

Cason

Man, Persia head game was out of this world, but I gotta stay away from that. If Nique find out it was her, all hell gon' break loose, I thought as I pulled up to Dahlia's house.

190

I'd been fucking with her for about a year now. I have love for her, but my heart belongs to Nique.

It's not fair to her for me to hold up her life when I have no intentions on ever leaving Nique, so I came over here to end it. I let myself in and found Dahlia in the kitchen. She had on one of my t-shirts with some boy shorts and her hair was in a messy ponytail. The sight of her ass in them boy shorts had a nigga dick on brick.

I know that's not what I came over here for, but it was something about her that the slightest thing turned me on. I walked up behind her, wrapped my arms around her waist, and kissed her neck.

"Hey, daddy, I didn't know you were coming over today," she greeted me.

"Do I have to call before I come now?" I asked.

"No, baby, I just wasn't expecting you. But I am happy you're here," she said as she kissed my lips softly then went back to cooking.

"Dinner is almost done so go relax and I will bring you your plate when it's done," she said, pushing me out of the kitchen.

Man, I loved that shit about her. She always catered to a nigga and made me feel like a king. It was gon' be hard to let her go but I gotta do what's right. I went in the den and tried to call Nique, but I still didn't get an answer.

I'm going to fuck Persia up when I see her. That shit she pulled wasn't cool. My dick jumped a little at the thought of her lips wrapped around my dick, but I shook those thoughts away and called Keys for an update. I also filled him in on what happened at the club last night.

Just as I was hanging up, my boo came in with my plate and

something for me to drink. Then she disappeared. I ate my food, put my plate in the kitchen, and then went to talk to her. She was in the shower so I lay across the bed and waited for her to get out. When she came in the room, I sat up

"Let me holla at you, Dahlia," I said as I patted the spot next to me.

She reluctantly came and sat down. This shit was hard for me. I looked into her pretty brown eyes and realized that I loved her, but I wasn't in love with her.

"Baby, this has got to end. I love you, but I am in love with Nique," I said as looked into her eyes.

"Why the fuck... you know what, I can't be mad at you. I knew you weren't goin' to leave her for me. I knew what it was when we started this," she said with tears streaming down her face.

"Dahlia, look, I don't mean to hurt you. I'm sorry that I led you on. Thank you for understanding," I said as I wiped her tears away and kissed her.

That kiss was supposed to be my goodbye, but things went further.

Dahlia undressed me and sucked my dick as if her life depended on it. When I came in her mouth, she swallowed it all and got me back up. I picked her up and put her up against the wall and fucked her slow. Then I laid her down and beat that pussy up. I came so hard inside of her that we cried out together.

I laid there for a moment and held her as she cried. then I went to shower so I could go home and fix things with Nique.

When I left, I set my key on the table as I kissed her forehead, then I walked out the door with no intentions of returning.

Tonight I was going to come clean with Nique about Dahlia. I was taking that shit with Persia to my grave.

I stopped to check on my auntie. then I left and went home.

Nique wasn't there when I got there. I just figured she was still at the shop. But as it got later, I started to worry. With all the shit that was going on, now wasn't the time for her to be pulling this shit. I sat there smoking blunt after blunt, thinking about life. I was ready for a family. I was ready to have some mini-me's running around here. I had to get my girl back.

I was pulled from my thoughts by the ringing of my phone. I looked at the caller ID and then answered.

"Yo, my man, it's time," I said to the caller and hung up.

Phoenix

Chapter 25

Farrah

Little miss prissy is really trying to be down. I wonder why she need money so bad. I know Amir ain't leave her broke. Let me find out my cousin treating her nose. Hmmm, I'ma have to play her real close, I thought as I checked my account balance. I was sitting on half a mill, but I wanted more. Just as that thought left my mind, an idea popped into my head.

Niggas gon' learn to follow orders when they are given, I thought as a sinister smile spread across my face. I still had a few hours to kill, so I decided to pamper myself before work. Maybe I would get lucky again.

Amina

Time was going by slowly and nervousness was setting in. Bitch, get it together. Maybe you won't have to take your clothes off, I tried to tell myself. But who was I kidding.

I called a moving company and they told me that they could come out in the morning, which was music to my ears.

The sooner I got out of the house, the better. An uneasy feeling came over me when my phone chimed, letting me know I had a message. I didn't want to open it, but it could've been Farrah so I checked it. To my surprise, it was Cas asking me to come over. He had something to talk to me about. I texted back and told him no can do because I was busy.

It must not have been too important because he didn't respond, which didn't bother me at all.

I started getting ready. I decided to do wet and wavy hair with a middle part. I set my hair and hopped in the shower.

Once I dried off and oiled my body, I started on my makeup. I did a subtle but dramatic look that made my eyes pop.

Once my makeup was to perfection, I laid out my clothes and lounged around for a little bit. I smoked a blunt, had a few shots, and got dressed.

I put on some black leggings that looked like they were painted on with a red corset. My shoes were red with a gold spike heel. Even though I had no intentions of taking my clothes off, I practiced some moves that didn't require a pole. Chino won't be able to tell me no once he sees all this ass clap.

Cason

I had a ring picked out two years ago, but I wasn't ready for that type of commitment.

Then I met Dahlia and I started feeling her. But seeing the pain I was causing Nique did something to me. I never thought she would think about leaving. She had stayed by my side through it all.

Nique was my heart and soul. I couldn't let her go. I shot Mina a text asking her to come holla at me, but she hit me with some bullshit. *Fuck she gotta do?* I thought. I didn't have time to figure out what her issue was.

I figured her and Nique must have been into it again. Hell, I was trying to fix my own shit, I didn't have time to fix theirs.

I needed to talk to somebody. My nigga wasn't around so I called Simeon.

"What's up, you busy?" I asked.

"Naw, not really, just chilling. What's good wit ya, Pla-ya-Playa?" he joked.

"You a funny dude, but on some real shit, I'm 'bout to settle down," I stated seriously.

"Yea right, not Mr. I'm-That-Nigga," he joked.

"I'm serious, man. I'm done with these hoes. I can't lose Nique over some bullshit so I'ma gon' head and pop that question," I said.

"Congrats, my nigga. So what happen?" he asked.

"Nigga, I let Persia suck my dick the other night and it was on Nique's voicemail," I said.

"Fuck outta here. how you let that shit happen?" he asked.

"Her head game is crazy, nigga. I forgot I was on the phone and shit," I said.

"She must've had you gone for you to slip up like that. I'm surprised your ass ain't in the hospital," he laughed.

"Shit, you too? Nigga, I thought for sure she was gon' tear some shit up," I laughed.

"Ain't her and P cool?" he inquired.

"Hell yea, but she didn't recognize her voice," I said relieved.

"Yea, you better keep that under wraps then, nigga," he said.

"I plan to. I'ma fuck P up tho 'cause that shit was foul," I said angrily.

"Fuck P, nigga, go get ya girl. I will get up wit ya tomorrow," he said and hung up.

I got my mind right and dipped out.

Simeon

Damn, I slept the whole day away, I thought after I got off the phone with Cas.

Keta was still lying next to me.

I hadn't slept that good in a long time. *I could get used to this,* I thought as I looked back at Keta, wishing she was Mina. But I shook that thought away as I got up. I went to handle my business in the bathroom.

I went to make us something to eat. While I was cooking, I called Ya-Ya to see if she had been handling her business. She was all business, no complaints about the baby or anything else.

I guess she got my message, I thought to myself as I felt Keta wrap her arms around my waist and kiss my neck.

That shit made a nigga dick jump. I ended my call with Ya-Ya. I set the table for us to eat and she kept staring at me like she was trying to figure me out.

"I want you to be my girl. I respect ya hustle, but I don't want you working at the club anymore," I said as I took a bite of my steak.

She sat there with a shocked expression as she let what I said sink in. Before I could say anything, my phone rang. I answered, "What's good?"

"Nigga, *we* got a mess to clean up," Hasaan said, sounding hype.

I excused myself and stepped outside.

"Fuck you mean *we*, nigga? Shit straight on my end," I barked.

"Nigga, that bitch is asking for more money," he said.

"Nigga, that's *your* problem. Fuck off my phone wit this shit," I barked.

I ended the call and went to roll up.

That nigga is so fucking stupid, I thought.

Keta came in the den with a drink and started massaging my shoulders after she sat it down on the table.

"So have you thought about what I asked you?" I asked.

"Yes and this all feels too good to be true, but I'ma throw

caution to the wind. Yes, I will be your girl," she stated with excitement and fear in her voice.

She's no Mina, but she will do for now, I thought as I nodded my head and blew smoke up in the air.

"Can you take me to the club so I can tell Chino I quit?" she asked.

"Yea, baby, now let's go get back in bed," I said as I picked her up and carried her upstairs.

Dominique

This nigga got a lot of fucking nerve. He didn't even look sorry, I thought as I checked into Chateau Armor.

I took my things to my room and tried to relax, but I had too much on my mind.

"I think it is time for me to let him go 'cause he is never goin' to do right by me. Why should I keep wasting my time on a nigga that would rather chase these hoes than be loyal to me?" I said to myself.

I didn't want to be alone with my thoughts so I went downstairs to the bar to have some drinks. I started off with three shots and a passion cocktail.

"Is this seat taken?" a sultry voice asked.

I shook my head no and went back to nursing my drink.

"I love this place. The food here is so delicious. Do you come here often?" the unknown woman asked.

"No, but every once in a while I like to spoil myself," I said.

"I know, girl. This place is a bit expensive but it is worth every penny," she gushed.

"It's even better when somebody else foots the bill. How 'bout we get a table and enjoy dinner and dessert on my no good ass man," I stated excitedly.

"My man dumped me today after two years. He walked away like it meant nothing. We used to come here a lot," she said.

"I'm sorry to hear that. My man cheated on me," I somberly stated.

"You seem to be handling it rather well. I know I would be a mess," she said.

"It has happened so many times that I am numb to it. I think this time I am done. I have had enough," I said.

"Girl my man left me for another woman. He *fucked* me one last time and walked out," she said as she took her drink to the head.

"Girl, he think he can buy me expensive shit and make everything okay. That shit don't heal my wounds," I said.

"I know what you mean, girl, that shit don't fix nothing. Your hair is cute. Who does it?" she asked.

"I do my own hair. That bracelet is cute. I have one just like it. My diamonds are canary yellow and pink. *My* man gave it to me for one of his many fuck ups," I said.

"My ex gave me this for our anniversary. What is the name of your shop?" she asked.

"Beautifully Yours. I'm usually there every day, just ask for Nique when you come in," I said.

"Okay, girl, I will. Well, I'ma get out of here. It was nice meeting you and thanks for dinner. We have to do this again," she said as she started to walk away. She turned around and said, "My name is Dahlia, but my friends call me Dee."

"Nice meeting you, Dee. Just let me know when and where," I said.

We parted ways and I went up to my room.

200

I lay across the bed wondering what was wrong with me. *Why wasn't I enough woman for him? What was it that I wasn't doing?* I thought.

I wanted to drown out my thoughts because I knew I was a damn good woman.

There was a man out there that would love to have a woman like me in his life. I didn't deserve this shit. I was leaving his no good ass.

If he wants these hoes he can have them. I'm done, I thought as I stumbled to the mini bar and grabbed all of the bottles of tequila out of it and knocked them back one after the other.

"Fuck you, Cason James," I yelled as tears streamed down my face. I laid there until sleep finally set in.

Phoenix

202

Chapter 26

Cason

I knew Nique was at Chateau Armor. She loved that hotel. I took her there for our first anniversary because I couldn't afford to take her to Paris at the time. Damn near broke a nigga, back then I was just getting deep into this shit but it was worth it to see her reaction.

Nique had been down with a nigga for eight years. She never complained about the late nights or me missing for days at a time. She held me down. She kept me sane. I couldn't see myself without her.

I got to Chateau Amor and paid the clerk to make me a key to her room.

I let myself in and seen her sprawled across the bed along with all the bottles. I laughed a little. She was so sexy. I got undressed and laid next to her. I nuzzled up close to her, inhaling her scent. In that moment, I felt complete.

"Mmmm, leave me alone, Cason," she mumbled.

"Baby, I'm sorry," I said as I held her tighter.

"I'm not up for this shit. Just get the fuck out and let me sleep. Wait a minute, how the hell did you get in here, anyway?" she slurred, fully awake now.

"None of that matters, ma, get up so we can talk. I'm 'bout to order you something to eat. When you get out of the shower, we will talk, baby," I said.

"There is nothing to say. I'm leaving you. These hoes can have you. I am done competing. By the time I get out of the shower, you should be gone," she stated while holding her head and walking to the bathroom.

I wasn't giving up that easy. I let her have her moment. I called room service and ordered her all her favorites. The room service waiter helped me set everything up. When Nique got out of the shower, she was still pissed.

"Look, Cason, you made your choice. All this shit you're doing isn't going to fix it this time. I finally get it," she sadly stated.

"Baby, sit down and just hear me out," I pleaded.

"For what? What are you going to say different this time, huh? You let a bitch suck ya dick and left the shit on *my* voicemail. You have no respect for me or this relationship, so why the fuck should I continue to stay where I'm not wanted?" she asked.

"That shit never should've happened. I'm sorry you had to hear that, baby, I am. I know that every time I do this shit it hurts you, and I don't want to hurt you anymore. I ended it with her. I realized that I don't need these hoes 'cause you are all the woman I need," I said.

"So what, her sucking your dick was goodbye? Man, get the fuck outta here. *You* don't know how to be faithful. *You* never have been and I held on this long 'cause *I* thought you would change. But I thought wrong. I'm done loving you 'cause all you do is hurt me. This isn't love. You don't love me. You love the streets and these hoes," she yelled.

"I love you. Dominique, these hoes don't mean shit to me. I'm done with that shit. I put that on my heart, baby. I'm done. You can't stop loving a nigga. You're the one that keeps me sane. I can't see my life without you. Will you marry me?" I asked her as I slid the ring on her finger.

There was a moment of silence as we looked into each other's eyes. I saw a single tear fall from her eye. As I wiped it away, I repeated, "Will you marry me?"

"Promise me you're done. Promise you won't hurt me again," she said.

"I promise," I said sincerely.

"*Yes. Yes. Yes,* I will marry you," she exclaimed.

She jumped into my lap and kissed me with so much passion it took my breath away. I carried her to the bed and laid her down. I grabbed a strawberry and traced her lips with it. Then I made a trail down her body. I rubbed it against her clit for a little bit. Then I put it in her pussy.

I took the ready whip and put some on her pussy, followed by some warm chocolate syrup. I drizzled it from her lips to her clit. I admired how sexy she looked as I took off my shirt and slowly licked and kissed her lips.

I worked my way down, sucking each nipple. Then I looked up into her eyes as I kissed her clit. She inhaled sharply and closed her eyes.

"Open 'em, look at me," I said. Then I went back to kissing and sucking on her clit.

I knew she was on the edge so I stopped and slowly licked up and down her pussy, sticking my tongue in her slowly in search of the strawberry.

"*Ooo* Casssssssss," she moaned as I sped up, going in deeper.

I sucked the strawberry out of her. I kissed her lips, sharing her sweetness with her before I went back down to finish her. I tongue fucked her slow, then fast.

"Oooooo. Casonnnnnnn. Casoonnnnnn. Ahhhhh yessssss, baby. Right. There," she moaned as she moved her hips to match my rhythm.

I held her in place and tongue fucked her faster.

"Dadddy, please let me cum. *Ooh god,* let me cum," she exclaimed.

I shook my head no as latched onto her clit and finger fucked her.

"Shit, oh god, I'm, I'm 'bout... Ohhhh god, I'm cumminggg." she breathlessly screamed as she squirted all over my face.

I licked up every drop. Then I entered her slowly, not giving her any time to recover.

I pushed all ten inches into her and didn't move, I just looked at her.

"Casonnnnnnn," she moaned.

"What, baby?" I asked.

"Make love to me," she moaned.

I put her legs in the crook of my arms and slowly moved my dick in and out, never breaking our eye contact. She was scratching my back, kissing me, and winding her hips to match my stroke.

"Aaaaahhh fuck, I love you, Nique," I exclaimed as I went deeper, picking up the pace.

"Awwwww shit, Casonnnnnn, Casonnnnn, oooooh daddy, I'm cumming," she screamed out as her pussy creamed on my dick.

I made slow love to her in every position until she tapped out at about 1am.

I was satisfied and happy because I got my girl back.

I sat on the balcony for a minute, smoked a blunt, and thought about Dahlia.

I kind of missed shorty but I knew what I was doing wasn't fair to her.

I watched Nique sleep through the window. then I went in and laid down next to her.

Clappers
Amina

You can do this. This is for Amir. You can't let him down, I told myself as I finally pulled into Clappers parking lot.

I had to do this because some shit wasn't adding up. Amir was set up.

I had been sitting in the parking lot for almost an hour. I checked my makeup again. Then I finally got out of the car.

The club was jumping. It was just as many females in there as it was men. I looked around for Farrah but I didn't see her. I saw a big booty red bone coming from the back.

"Excuse me, can you tell me where I can find Far... I mean Persia," I asked.

She made a face and then walked off.

Damn, she could've told me where to find her, I thought as I walked to the back where the red bone had just come from. I was getting some less than friendly stares, which didn't faze me.

If these hoes were up on their shit, then my presence wouldn't be a threat.

I spotted my cousin talking to an Asian chick.

This girl made me do a double take, her beauty was breathtaking. She was built like Farrah, just a lil bit thicker.

"Well look who finally decided to show up. Jade, this is my cousin I was telling you about," Persia said.

"I told you I would be here. Nice to meet you, Jade. I'm Duchess," I said.

"I'm scared of you, honey. Come on so I can introduce you to Chino. You cutting into my money time," Persia said with a giggle.

As we walked through the club, men and women were slapping my ass and asking for lap dances.

When we got to Chino's office, I let Persia do all the talking as he gave me a once over and motioned for me to turn around.

"P, you know I don't need no more dancers right now, but I can't let all that ass get away. How 'bout you work the bar? I will pay you a thousand a week and you keep all your tips. How does that sound?" he said.

"When do I start?" I eagerly asked.

"Tonight if you like. What's your name, sexy lady?" he asked.

"Duchess," I replied.

"P, take her to the bar and tell Gina to show her the ropes. Before you leave for the night, I need to holla at you 'bout something, Farrah," Chino said.

Persia just nodded her head and exited the office.

"Well, baby girl, welcome to Clappers. I will come check on every once and a while. Watch these hoes 'cause they will try you. Gina, this is Duchess. Show her the ropes," she said, and then walked away.

Gina didn't have to show me too much. I mean it wasn't rocket science. We were just making drinks.

Gina didn't look too thrilled about me being there, so I did my own thing.

I was watching the redbone from earlier do her thang on the pole. I felt like she was dancing to the wrong song but, other than that, her show was good.

I was standing behind the bar making my ass clap to the beat in my own world because Gina was doing all the work.

"Aye, ma, come clap that ass over here," some dude with a Mohawk yelled.

"Sweetheart, I don't see any money in ya hands. You're better off watching my ass from a distance," I said.

"Ma, money is no issue, believe that," he said as he pulled out a couple bands.

I slowly walked over there, turned around, and before I could start, he stopped me.

"Naw, ma, hop ya thick ass up on the bar and make that ass clap for me," he said.

"Girl, you can't do that. Chino don't allow us to dance. We only serve drinks," Gina said.

I was wondering where the hell she came from because last I checked, she was in some dark skin nigga face showing her 32s for a tip.

I ignored her and hopped on the bar. I turned around and made my ass clap in dude's face.

"Damn, ma, why you back here and not up there?" he asked as he handed me a wad of money.

I slipped it in my bra.

"That's something you would have to ask my boss. What you drinking tonight?" I asked once I hopped down off the bar.

"Shit, you, if you let me," he flirted.

"Sorry, I'm not on the menu. But if I was, you couldn't handle all off this," I flirted.

"Duchess, is my little brother bothering you?" Chino asked as he walked up and gave his brother dap.

"No, he was just complimenting me and giving me his drink order," I said as I walked away to get his bottles.

I don't know what he's drinking, but he is going to drink whatever I give him, I thought as I grabbed two bottles of Belvedere.

"That shit you pulled wasn't cute. You gon' give me half of whatever he gave you. We spilt our tips up here," Gina whispered harshly.

"I am not giving you shit. I suggest you earn some or turn some tricks to get ya pockets laced," I said. Then I bumped her shoulder and went back to my customer. He was still talking to Chino when I walked up. I handed him the bottles.

"This is for you, sexy," he said as he gave me two bills and walked away, disappearing into the crowd.

The club was live.

I saw a lot of familiar faces while I was making drinks and getting bottles.

After the initial shock wore off, they would offer their condolences and then promise to give me the world if I would be their girl.

My night was running smoothly. I was enjoying myself and making money at the same time. *I could get used to this,* I thought as I flirted with some nigga and his girl.

Chapter 27

Marketa

I was excited. I finally had somebody that I could call my own. This seemed too good to be true. *I don't know what this nigga is up to but I'ma enjoy it while I can,* I thought as he carried me upstairs. I was finally about to be in the same circle as Amina. I couldn't wait to see her face. *I need to call Mika and see if she can keep Paris another night,* I thought.

"Baby, before you start the movie, I need to tell you something. I have a five year old daughter, Paris. If you can't handle that, I understand," I said as I silently prayed that he didn't change his mind.

"I can't wait to meet my daughter, baby," he said.

I was stuck. I wasn't expecting that answer.

"You really aren't like other men. Baby, I'm 'bout call my neighbor and check on my daughter," I said as I dialed Mika's number.

"Hey, Mika, how's my baby?" I spoke cheerily.

"Girl, she good, running 'round here wit Shan. Keta, what you want 'cause you don't ever call to check to her," she spoke with agitation.

"Why I gotta want something, Mika, damn? Girl, you know I stay calling to check on her, you silly," I stated playfully as the guilt hit my heart because she was right. I was trying to save face in front of Simeon.

"Girl, your ass don't even... You know what, Keta, get to the point 'cause I gotta get dinner started," she said.

"Is it okay if she stays another night or two 'cause I don't know when I'm coming home," I asked.

"Mmm hmm," she said. Then she hung up on me.

I didn't give a fuck about how she felt. all I cared about at this moment was this sexy ass nigga, my sexy ass nigga, laying in this bed wanting me.

I crawled down his body slowly.

When I was face to face with his dick, I pulled it out of the slit in his boxers and put it all in my mouth.

I watched him close his eyes as he inhaled sharply.

I made love to him with my mouth slowly for lil bit then I took his dick out of my mouth and held it firmly as I slapped my tongue and jaws with it. I licked it like a lollipop, sucking firmly on the head. I did this over and over.

I felt his body tense up so I put his dick back in my mouth. I damn near choked but I relaxed my throat and took him all the way in, over and over, until I felt his nut going down my throat.

I went to brush my teeth and get a warm washcloth. Once I was done taking care of my hygiene, I cleaned him up. Then I lay down next to him.

We slept until midnight. then we showered and headed to the club.

When we got there, the club was packed for it to only be Thursday.

Simeon got us a table and I went to get our drinks.

As I walked through the club, niggas were asking me if I was working tonight. I shook my head no and kept it moving.

When I got to the bar, I thought my eyes had to be playing tricks on me because I knew that wasn't who I thought it was.

"What's up, Gina?" I said.

"Hey, Xstasy. What you drinking?" she asked.

"Let the new girl handle this, G," I said.

She walked away to go get her. *I'll be damned if it isn't Miss My-Shit-Don't-Stink herself, Amina,* I thought as she walked towards me.

"Oh how the mighty have fallen. I guess shit wasn't so sweet after all, huh?" I said with a smirk on my face.

"Bitch, don't think 'cause I'm behind this bar that I won't whoop your ass. Ain't shit changed so I advise you to place your order or move the fuck on," she said with a smile on her face but death in her eyes.

I looked her up and down as I thought about trying her, but I didn't want to get embarrassed in front of my man so I placed my order, got my drinks, and stormed off.

I slammed the drinks on the table and flopped down next to Simeon.

"I can't stand that bitch," I huffed.

"What's wrong, baby?" Simeon asked.

"That bitch, Amina, working the bar. She lucky I didn't beat her ass," I said, and then took a sip of my drink.

"What you mean working the bar?" he asked too concerned for me.

"She making drinks and shaking her ass at the bar. Why do you care?" I asked.

"Don't come at with the bullshit, *Marketa.* Go holla at Chino so we can be out," he said.

I did as I was told and went to go find Chino.

Simeon

213

I was pissed just thinking about these niggas looking at Mina. I wanted to go see the shit for myself but I knew if I did, I would snatch her ass up. She didn't need to be in here dancing and shit.

She know that if she needed anything, me or Cas would give it to her. She is set tho, so why is she working here? I thought as I downed my drink.

It took everything in me not to check Keta for disrespecting her like that.

I saw that nigga Hasaan and sent him a drink. That nigga was gon' let these bitches kill him.

I hope he handled that shit wit ol' girl. Hell, he lucky it was me she came to and not that nigga Cas cause his ass would be missing right now, I thought.

I grabbed my phone and sent a few pics. Then I laid back and let some thick dark skin chick give me a lap dance.

Dominique

I woke up at about two looking at my ring in awe. I never thought he was serious about getting married. I mean we talked about it. But I felt like he was just saying that shit to entertain me, especially since he was still out there doing him.

I rolled over and watched him sleep. He was so damn sexy. My pussy was soaking wet and I owed him for putting my ass to sleep.

I put my head under the covers and started kissing his dick lightly. It jumped with each kiss. I kissed his balls, licked up his shaft, and then gently sucked on his head. I took more of him in my mouth each time until I felt his dick in my throat. I sucked a little firmer and faster, taking him to the edge. Then I would go slow.

"Ahhhhh, Nique," he moaned as I worked on his dick. "Shittt, baby, let me cum. Fuckkk, let me cum," he begged.

I shook my head no as I deep throated his dick over and over.

"Suck it just like that, mmmmm shit," he moaned as I sucked faster.

Then I stopped and hopped on his dick. I rocked back and forth slowly. He gripped my hips, trying to make his dick go deeper.

"I'm cumminggggg, ooohh, I'm cumminggggg, ooooohhhhh," I screamed as I creamed on his dick.

I was in heaven riding his dick. I felt another orgasm coming as I bounced up and down on it. I bounced harder and faster and he met me thrust for thrust.

"Ssss, right there, right there. I love you. Shittttt, I lovvvveeee you," I moaned.

"Fuck, I love you too, shit. Fuck, I'm 'bout to cum," he exclaimed.

I went harder, making my pussy contract on his dick as he thrusted in and out of my pussy.

"Fuckkkk," we screamed in unison as we both came.

I collapsed on his chest, trying to catch my breath. Our hearts were beating in sync as our breathing slowed down. I felt my eyes getting heavy but his dick was still hard. I slowly started moving up and down. Then he flipped me onto my stomach and entered me from behind. He started off with deep slow thrusts.

"*Mmmm, shit, Casonnn. Cas. Casss,*" I moaned as he went deeper.

"Throw that ass back on this dick," he said as he began to pound my pussy.

I was throwing it back, taking every angry thrust he dished out. I came all over his dick. As he pulled my hair, he kept going faster and deeper.

I tried to run but he grabbed my hips and held me in place until he let out a loud groan releasing his seeds deep into my womb.

We collapsed on the bed. He fell asleep instantly.

I can't wait to tell Mina, I thought as I snuggled closer to him and fell asleep.

Farrah

I was keeping an eye on Mina. She was handling herself well for this to be her first night. I saw Simeon come in with Keta so I assumed Cas would be in momentarily. But as time progressed, I didn't see him.

I peeped Hasaan in the cut so I sent him a drink and a lap dance. I smirked as I watched Jade do her thang.

"What's up, girl? You working tonight?" I said as I gave Keta a hug.

"Naw, girl, my man said I can't shake my ass no more. I hit the jackpot, bitchhhhh," she said with a giggle.

"I see you, boo. Do your thang, ma, but make sure you got a backup plan just case that nigga start tripping," I said.

"Girl, I feel you. Well let me go holla at Chino so I can get my man outta here," she said as she hugged me.

I told her to keep in touch and went on about my business. I was walking around doing lap dances. I hit the stage a few times. Then I went to go holla at Chino.

"What's good, boss man?" I asked as I sat on his desk.

"Shit, what's up wit ya girl Cherry?" he asked, looking at me sideways.

"I haven't heard from her," I confidently spoke.

"Mmm hmm, well take a look at this," he said as he hit play on the DVD player.

What appeared on the screen made my heart stop.

"How much you want for it, Chino?" I asked.

"How much you want for it, Chino?" he said mocking me as he approached me.

"I had to do what I had to do. It was either *me or her,*" I said.

"Bitch, this my *shit. My* livelihood. I make millions a fucking night in here and it ain't from you popping that stank ass pussy either, hoe. Had *I* not cleaned up *your* mess, my shit could've been fucked up. So I own your ass indefinitely. Now put that hot ass mouth to work," he ordered as he forced me down on my knees.

I didn't mind sucking his dick. Chino's dick was beautiful, it curved to the right and his nut was sweet like caramel.

He didn't have to force me. But, hey, I'm a freaky bitch so all this shit did was turn me on. I sucked his dick like my life depended on it until he shot his sweet nut down my throat. I swallowed it all and went back to work.

Damn, how the fuck am I gon' get that video? And when did he put a camera in our dressing room? I thought as I walked to the bar and knocked back a few shots.

Chino must not know who the fuck I am, I mentally hyped myself up. *I don't take threats lightly and I'ma have to feed this nigga to the wolves.*

"Persia, I need to holla at you. Let's do breakfast," Duchess said as she cleaned the bar.

"A'ight, I'm about to go change," I said and headed to the dressing room.

Amina

Damn, I made six stacks on my first night. Not bad, I thought to myself. I saw Farrah coming out of the club so I told her to meet me at Waffle House.

I guess everybody from the club had the same idea because half of them were there. Thankfully, most of them were getting their stuff to go.

I grabbed a table and waited for Farrah to come in. While I was waiting, Chino's brother came over to the table.

"Hi, beautiful, my name is Calico and yours?" he asked after he kissed my hand.

Blushing, I said, "Duchess."

"That's a sexy ass name. Why are you working at Clappers?" he asked.

"Thank you. Paying my way thru law school," I lied. He didn't need to know the real reason.

"Co, why you over here bothering my cousin?" Farrah asked Calico when she walked up.

"Persia, what's good? I didn't know she was your fam. I was just getting to know her tho," he said as he got up to let her sit down.

"Duchess, can I take you out to dinner?" he asked.

"Maybe, give me your number," I said.

I put his number in my phone and he walked back over to his table.

I was daydreaming as I watched him walk back to his table. Calico was about 5'8" with a smooth milk chocolate baby face and coffee colored eyes. He put me in the mind of the rapper Jim Jones.

I was in a daze. He appeared to be a little bowlegged.

"What are you thinking about, Mina?" Farrah asked as she jarred me from my thoughts.

"Nothing major, girl," I said, taking a sip of my water.

"Your ass lusting after Calico. You ain't slick," she giggled. "I got two tickets to San Juan waiting on me and I wanted to know if you wanted to join me. I'm leaving after I make an appearance at the funeral, which is at ten o'clock am today. The flight leaves at one," I said, ignoring what she said.

"Hell yea, I'm there. Let me get home so I can pack. I will see you at the funeral. Are you riding with his mom?" she asked.

"Naw, cause I am not hanging around long. I have a flight to catch," I nonchalantly stated.

She gave me a perplexed looked that I brushed off. I finished my meal and left.

I checked my phone once I was in the car and there was a message from Maine and two from that unknown number.

Maine's message was sweet but I knew it was bullshit. I sent him a text letting him know that I would see him tonight.

I read the message from the unknown person it said, *Beware of wolves in sheep's clothing.*

I was about to throw my phone on the seat when a picture came through of that baby sleeping. The caption read: *See you soon mommy.*

I don't know who this bitch is but she is smart to hide her identity. I hope she don't think I'm about to play mommy to her bastard ass son 'cause she gon be in for a rude awakening. Reading that message removed all the guilt I felt about what I was about to do.

Phoenix

Chapter 28

The Funeral
Amina

As soon as I walked into the church, the guilt crept back in.

No matter how much Amir had hurt me, I still loved him.

I slowly walked to the front of the church. I took a deep breath before I looked at his body.

He looked so handsome and peaceful. I stroked his cheek and kissed him goodbye as I placed the ring he gave me in his hands.

I embraced his mother, not bothering to acknowledge Nique or Cas, then I took my seat.

The turnout was amazing. Everybody who was some-body was there to pay their last respects.

I didn't plan on speaking, but I heard a baby cry out and it compelled me to speak.

"Amir was and will always be the love of my life. He was not a perfect man, but he was good man. He loved many of the women here, but I knew I was his heart. well that is what I believed. Amir would've been a great father but because of greed, deceit, and pure jealousy, the people closest to him stabbed him in the back and robbed him of his life," I solemnly stated. But before I could finish, I was interrupted.

"What you trying to say, Mina?" Cas said looking up at me.

"I'm not trying to say anything. I made it perfectly clear, *Mr. James,*" I said.

"I won't be needing these anymore. I know you were going to come claim everything that wasn't nailed down so I saved you the trouble," I said as I tossed the keys to Ms. Cynthia and put my sunglasses on.

I proceeded to step down and make my exit, but Nique stopped me in my tracks with a hard slap to the face.

"After all my cousin did for you, this how you do him, huh?" she asked as she attempted to charge me but Cason grabbed her.

I rubbed my cheek and laughed in her face.

"Bitch, you lucky I have a flight to catch. Hear this tho, the next time you put your hands on *me,* you and your cousin gon' be reunited," I calmly said as I put my sunglasses back on and fixed my hair.

I walked out of the church with my head held high and Farrah right behind me. We got in my car. I turned up the music because I wasn't up for the third degree, and headed to the airport.

Dominique

I can't believe this bitch had the audacity to get her ass up there and talk out the side of her neck about my cousin, threaten me, and then she fixed her fucking mouth to insinuate that Cason set up Amir, his best friend since the sandbox, 'cause he was jealous. the nerve if that bitch, I thought as I tried to get out of Cas's hold.

"I really can't believe that she would disrespect my family this way. Then she gon' threaten me, after all the shit we've been thru, she threatened me. That bitch better kill me first 'cause *every* fucking time I see her I'ma beat her ass," I fumed to Cas.

"She ain't in her right mind right now, baby. She..." he said.

"I *don't* give a fuck what frame of mind she is in. she ain't the only one who hurting," I yelled as I broke free and stormed out of the church.

I stood outside trying to regain my composure so that I could be strong for my aunt because she loved that girl like a daughter. She would never do her any harm.

It seemed like time was at a standstill as I watched them carry Amir's casket out of the church. Everybody was coming out, going to their cars so that we could go to the grave site when a hail of gunfire sent us all running for cover.

Cason

I can't believe this shit, I thought as I started dumping shots at the niggas who were dumping shots at us.

Did they think we wasn't gon be strapped? Funeral or not, we know how the game is played and we stay on point. But to shoot up my nigga funeral is disrespect at the highest level.

Once again, my nigga was laid out in the street with his body riddled with bullets. I went to make sure my girl and her aunt were good.

"Keys, find these niggas like yesterday. Simeon, call Wop and y'all niggas know what time it is," I said as I went back in the church in search of my girl and her aunt.

I found them in the sanctuary comforting each other with a few other family members. I told them to stay put until I came back to get them. Once I knew they were good, I went outside and picked up my nigga's body and put him back in his casket.

I was pacing in front of the church trying to figure out who the fuck would be so foolish to do some shit like this. *I'm personally handling this shit 'cause this was disrespectful and I'm not letting this shit ride. I'ma take everything away from these niggas,* I thought as I dialed Simeon's number.

"Aye, make sure she miss that flight and bring her ass to me like yesterday," I calmly stated, and then ended the call. I made sure everybody was good. Then I took Nique and Ma Dukes home.

Amina

This little vacation is just the thing I need after all the bullshit I've been thru, I thought as I parked my car.

We sat there and smoked one. When we got out the car to get our luggage, we were stopped by Simeon.

"Ladies, please make this easy. Just get in the car. Today has been long enough and I am asking y'all nicely," he said with that sexy ass smile as he crossed his arms.

"I must have hurt Cason's feelings for him to send you. Tell your boss that his feelings don't mean shit to me and I will deal with him when I get back," I firmly stated as I opened my trunk. Simeon just stood there patiently waiting on me to follow orders, but that wasn't going to happen.

I don't have time for his lil temper tantrum. Hell, if he felt some kind of way he should've spoke up when I was at the church, I thought as I grabbed my carryon and placed it on my shoulder.

"Amina, I'm trying to be nice," he said calmly.

"Mina, just get in the car. We can catch a later flight," Farrah said.

"No, fuck him and his boss. I'm not getting in the car and that's final," I spoke loudly.

"Get the fuck in the car, now. You should've have listened to your little friend," he gritted as he snatched me up, threw me in the car, and slammed the door.

"Can I get her keys please, sexy?" Farrah flirtingly asked.

"Naw, lil mama, you goin' too. So get ya lil ass in the car too," he told Farrah.

She looked like she wanted to object but I guess he gave her a *don't fuck wit me* type look and she got her ass in the car.

Simeon

This nigga could have done this shit on his own. He gon' quit playing me like I'ma flunky ass nigga. I'ma show him how to run shit for real.

He got all these bloodclot ass niggas running around here like they kings when onli one can wear di crown. I'ma rule wit an iron fist. Niggas and bitches will fear me and flock to me.

He got me chasing down a bitch when he should be gunning for any and every nigga that they had, have, or could potentially have problems with, I thought as I checked Mina out in the rearview mirror.

She was so sexy when she was mad. *Lil mama got heart.*

Amir trained her well, but that mouth of hers gon' get her fucked up.

My phone ringing took me out of my thoughts. Ya-Ya's name appeared on the caller ID. my first thought was *what this bitch want now.*

"What's good?" I gritted.

"Nigga, you coming to get this baby is what's good," she fussed.

"I told you there will be a ticket waiting for you in an hour, bitch," I gritted, then ended the call so that I could call dumb ass to have him go pick her ass up from the airport.

"Yo, nigga, rude gurl and lil man will be back tonight. Pick her up. I will hit you with the info," I said.

Unbeknownst to me, Farrah was taking it all in trying to decipher what everything meant.

Farrah

Damn, I was looking forward to San Juan. Oh well, I hope this shit don't take all night 'cause I could go make some money tonight, I thought as I checked our kidnapper out on the sly.

I slightly giggled to myself. I would love to be kidnapped by him any day. He probably know how to mmmmm. I clenched my legs together as his phone started ringing.

I glanced at the caller ID to see if I knew the person calling but I didn't. I made a mental note of the name tho. I was ear hustling on his conversation and was instantly turned off 'cause I don't do baby mama drama, nor do I do kids.

I tuned him out until he made his next call and I heard the voice on the other end.

Why the hell is he talking to Hasaan? More importantly, does he know that they killed Amir? I silently questioned myself.

What the hell is goin' on here? I need to talk to Cas. Hell, was he in on it, too? I thought as I glanced back at Mina.

Cason

I looked at my girl and ma dukes and thought about how close I came to losing them.

My nigga would have lost it if something would have happened to either one of them.

Damn, Amir used to be the mastermind when it came to this war shit. He was always plotting and planning. but fuck all that, I'm shooting first and asking questions later, I told myself as I pulled up in front of the hotel.

"I'm not staying here, Cason. Take me home, now. I'm not about to let some wannabe ass gangstas run me from my home," Cynthia firmly stated

"Ma, it's just for tonight. Until I make sure it is safe, you're not going home. No disrespect, but I will carry your ass inside if I have to," I told her.

She let out a deep sigh as they both got out of the car.

I made sure they were straight. Then I went to check on my spots and peep a few scenes. My first stop was to Smoke's old spots.

His peeps were suspect because of what happened the other day at the meeting.

Then there was that nigga Debo and his lil whack ass crew. That nigga was talking big shit, plus he was short ten stacks.

Nigga probably hanging on his own nuts cause he think he got over.

"Yo, go level all that shit and bring that nigga Debo to the tracks. I got something special planned for his ass," I told Wop with a smirk on my face.

Once I was done dealing with them niggas, I went to go see what the fuck was up with Mina's slick talking ass.

Amina

I texted Maine and told him I wouldn't be able to make it but thanks anyway. I knew that wherever Simeon was taking us wasn't goin to be a quick trip.

I should have never went to his funeral, I thought as we pulled up at secluded house.

"Get out," Simeon demanded.

We reluctantly got out of the car, unfazed by his tone.

Farrah

This is going to work out in my favor. I can make it look like goody two shoes set this whole thing up. I wonder if I put my skills down, will he let me in on the plan, I thought to myself as I watched Simeon seal his blunt.

I walked up to him slowly, grabbing the blunt from between his fingers. I placed it between my lips and turned around sensually moving my body like a snake as I leaned back into him. I looked up into his eyes holding his gaze as he lit the blunt. I inhaled deeply allowing the smoke to fill my lungs. I blew it out of my mouth, allowing the rest to come out of nose. Then I asked, "Why did you set Amir up?"

He dropped the lighter and placed his hand around my throat firmly squeezing it.

I looked into his hooded death filled eyes with a smile and I whispered, "If we work together, I can make sure you're the last man standing."

He looked as if he contemplated what I said right as a gun was placed at the back of his head.

To Be Continued...
The Ultimate Betrayal 2
Coming Soon

Phoenix

SLEEPING IN HEAVEN, WAKING IN HELL **I, II & III**
By **Forever Redd**
THE DEVIL WEARS TIMBS **I, II & III**
and BURY ME A G **1 & II**
By **Tranay Adams**
DON'T FU#K WITH MY HEART **I & II**
By **Linnea**
BOSS'N UP **I & II**
By **Royal Nicole**
A DANGEROUS LOVE **I, II, III, IV, V & VI**
By **J Peach**
CUM FOR ME
An **LDP Erotica Collaboration**
THE KING CARTEL
By **Frank Gresham**
STREET JUSTICE **I & II**
By **Chance**
THESE NIGGAS AIN'T LOYAL **I & II**
BY **Nikki Tee**
A HUSTLA'Z AMBITION **I & II**
By **Damion King**
SILVER PLATTER HOE
By **Reds Johnson**
LOYALTY IS BLIND
By **Kenneth Chisholm**

<u>BOOKS BY LDP'S CEO, CA$H</u>

TRUST NO MAN
TRUST NO MAN 2
TRUST NO MAN 3
BONDED BY BLOOD
SHORTY GOT A THUG
A DIRTY SOUTH LOVE
THUGS CRY
THUGS CRY 2
TRUST NO BITCH
TRUST NO BITCH 2
TRUST NO BITCH 3
TIL MY CASKET DROPS

Coming Soon
THUGS CRY 3
BONDED BY BLOOD 2
TRUST NO BITCH (KIAM & EYEZ' STORY)